THE SPLENDID FAIRING

(Femina-Vie Heureuse Prize)

By

CONSTANCE HOLME

'*All night long the water is crying to me*'

Geoffrey Cumberlege
OXFORD UNIVERSITY PRESS
London New York Toronto

The Splendid Fairing *was first published in* 1919.
It was first included in The Worlds Classics *in* 1933,
and was reprinted in 1934, 1935, 1944, 1947 *and* 1951.

PRINTED IN GREAT BRITAIN

416
THE SPLENDID
FAIRING

CONTENTS

SIMON AND SARAH

I

PERHAPS it would never have happened but for the day. A brave, buoyant day, with a racing wind, might have scattered the clinging obsession just in time. A tender, laughing day might have laid a healing finger on old sores. A clean, frosty day might have braced the naturally sane old mind. But Fate, out of all the days in the year, took upon itself to send just this.

The human soul, which seems so utterly out of reach, is only shut away from every other soul. In every other respect it is like a harp hung on a tree. Even the actual day as it comes is itself a lever in many a fate. Deeds are done on certain days which on others would be mere passing impulses easily dead before the night. This blind Martinmas Day went all day long with its head among the clouds, as if it thought that never again would there be any sun. Indeed, it was out of the lack of every sort of sight that the evil grew; since, otherwise—'Mothers couldn't have done those things,' as Geordie would have said.

All day the earth retained that stillness which it keeps as a rule only for the last hour before the dawn. Everywhere in the morning there was mist—that strange, wandering, thinking mist that seems to have nothing to do with either earth or air; and when the slow dark drew back there would be mist everywhere again. Between those shadowy tide-marks of the air there was a space when the white mist shredded above the trees,

B

leaving the atmosphere with the look of a glass that has been breathed upon and never clears.

The Simon Thornthwaites were going to market simply because they did not know how to stay away. They went as naturally as the sun comes out of the east, but with a good deal less of decision about the journey. They looked dull and tired, too, less indeed as if they were setting out than as if they were wearily trundling home again. Both horse and trap looked as though they might fall to pieces after an extra jolt, and the jumble of harness was mended here and there with string. There was neither butter nor fowl in the market-basket behind; there was not even a limp rabbit dangling over the wheel. But all the time they were part of a chain which gave them a motive and impulse not their own, since others, more sure of their errand, were taking the same road. Sometimes a horseman on a young Shire went past with a flash of feather and a clumping of hoofs. Livelier traps spun by at a trot and gave them a hail. Behind and before them they had an occasional glimpse of the procession stretching to the town.

They had climbed from the marsh, leaving it dropped like a colourless cloth beside the sea, and already they seemed to have been a long time on the road. They had not slept much, and, waking, had had the cheated feeling, common to the weary, that the foregoing day had never really ended nor the incoming morning ever quite begun. Indeed, the strange, dreamlike day had never really seemed to come awake. Looking back and west, they saw everything grey, with just a lightened shadow marking the far sea, and

the marsh lying down on its face like a figure
flung down to die. Houses sat low to the earth
as if they crouched, and the trees were vague
bodiless wisps, without backbone or sap. When
they had their first glimpse of Witham, they saw
the town on the fell-side like a fortress through
smoked glass, and the Castle alone on its hill was
of shadow-stones poised on a poised cloud.

The Simon Thornthwaites were old now, and
under-dogs in the tussle of life, but they had once
been as strong and confident as most. Sometimes
they had a vision of their former selves, and wondered how this could ever have been that. The
old man was thin and bent, the sort that shows
the flame through the lantern long before the
end, but the woman was stronger-boned, squarer,
and still straight. Most of her life she had worked
like a horse, but she was still straight. Her face
was mask-like and her mouth close. Only her
hands betrayed her at times—old, over-done
hands that would not always be still. Her eyes
seemed to look straight before her at something
only she could see—staring and staring at the
image which she had set up.

They farmed Sandholes down on the marsh, a
lonely bit of a spot that looked as if it had been
left there for a winter's tide to take away. It had
always had an unlucky name, and, like many
unlucky people and things, seemed to have the
trick of attracting to itself those who were equally
ill-starred. Certainly, Sandholes and the Thornthwaites between them had achieved amazing
things in the way of ill-luck. No doubt both farm
and folk would have done better apart, but then
they had never succeeded in getting apart. It

was just as if Fate had thrown and kept them
together in order to do each other down. Luck
to luck—there seemed nothing else to be said
about the Thornthwaites' plight. They even
carried the stamp of each other plain to be seen.
You had only to look at the farm to know how
its tenants looked; you had only to see the folk to
know what their home was like. Perhaps it was
just that the double weight of misfortune was too
big a thing to lift. Perhaps the canker at the
heart of it all would allow nothing to prosper
and grow sweet.

They had an easy landlord, easy and rich; too
easy and rich, perhaps, for the Thornthwaites'
good. That farm had money—landlord's and
tenant's—spent on it above its due; yes, and a
certain amount of borrowed brass as well. It had
work put into it, thought and courage sufficient
to run a colony, and good-will enough to build
a church. And all that it did in return was to go
back and back and be a deadhead and a chapter
of accidents and an everlasting disappointment
and surprise. It was a standing contradiction of
the saying—'Be honest with the land, and it will
be honest with you.' Everything went wrong
with that farm that could go wrong, as well as
other things that couldn't by any chance have
gone anything but right. Most people would
have thrown a stone at it at an early stage, but
it was part of the Thornthwaite doom that they
could not tear themselves away. Even when
there seemed no longer a reason for staying, still
they stayed. The one streak of sentiment in them
that survived the dismal years held them there
captive by its silken string.

But to-day, as they jogged and jolted endlessly towards Witham, the whole drear, lifelong business came to an end. No matter what they had thought of the probable future to themselves, they had hitherto shut their mouths obstinately and clung close. They had never even said to each other that some day they would have to quit. They had put it off so long that it seemed the least little push would always put it farther still. But to-day the matter suddenly settled itself for good; almost, it seemed, between one telegraph-post and the next.

Martinmas hirings would be in full swing when they got in, but there was no need now for Simon to enter the ring. Their hired man had seen them through the busiest time, but they could manage without him through the winter months. Their hired men had never stayed very long, because the depression of the place seemed to get into their bones. They tired of crops which seemed to make a point of 'finger and toe,' and of waiting through dismal weeks to get in the hay. Now the Thornthwaites would never have the worry of hay-time on their own account again—never open the door to catch the scent from their waiting fields—never watch the carts coming back in the golden evening to the barn. 'Never again' would be written over many things after to-day, but perhaps it was there that they saw it written first. After all this time things had somehow stopped of themselves, and after all this time there was nothing to do but go.

Lads and lasses went by them on cycles, or tugging bundles as they walked; youth with bright cheeks and strong shoulders and clear

eyes, taking its health and strength to the market
to be hired. Some of them greeted the old folks
as they passed, but others did not as much as
know their names. Both Simon and Sarah came
of old and respectable stock, but to the young
generation skimming by on wheels these two had
been as good as buried years ago. Sarah's eyes
strained themselves after the lithe bodies of the
lads, while Simon looked at the lasses with their
loads. He would have liked to have offered some
of them a lift, but he knew he would catch it from
Sarah if he did. Sarah hated the younger end of
folk, she always said, and the fly-away lasses she
hated most of all. She saw them going past her
into beautiful life, just as their swifter wheels
went past the trap. Always they were leaving
her behind as it seemed to her that she had always
been left. It was true, of course, that she had had
her turn, but now it seemed so far away it might
never have been. All she could see in the background when she looked behind was the cheerless
desert which she had had to cover since.

They were about half-way to Witham when
the moment of spoken decision caught them
unawares. All their stolid resistance and obstinate clinging to the farm gave in that instant as
easily as a pushed door. It was as if a rock at the
mouth of a cave had suddenly proved no more
than a cloud pausing before it in the act of drifting by. The end came as nearly always after
a prolonged fight—smoothly, painlessly, with a
curious lack of interest or personal will. The
burden had been so heavy that the last straw
passed almost unnoticed which brought them
finally to the ground. They had lived so close to

the edge for so many years that the step which carried them over it scarcely jarred.

They were climbing the long hill that runs from Doestone Hall, the Tudor house standing close to the cross-roads. By turning their heads they could see its gabled front with the larches set like lances beside its door. The river ran swift below the beech-covered slope of the park, reaching impatiently after the ebbed tide. The house, for all the weight of its age, looked unsubstantial in the filmy air. Fast as the river flowed below, from above it looked like a sheeted but still faintly moving corpse.

The road was damp and shadowy under the overhanging trees, and padded with the hoof-welded carpet of the autumn leaves. The fields on either side were formless and wet, and seemed to stretch away to unknown lengths. The hedges appeared to wander and wind across the land without purpose and without end. Under all the hedges and trees there were leaves, wet splashes of crushed colour on the misted grass. Simon lifted his whip to point at the hips and haws, and said it would be a hard winter when it came, but Sarah did not so much as turn her head.

'I'm bothered a deal wi' my eyes, Simon,' she said in a quiet tone. 'I thought I'd best see doctor about 'em to-day.'

He dropped his gaze from the hedges with a startled stare. 'Oh, ay? That's summat fresh, isn't it?' he enquired. 'You've never said nowt about it afore.'

'Nay, what, I thought it was likely just old age. But I've gitten a deal worse these last few weeks. I can't shape to do a bit o' sewing or owt.'

'Ay, well, you'd best see doctor right off,' Simon said, and the horse crawled a little farther up the hill. They did not speak again for some time, but those who live together in a great loneliness grow to speak together in thought as much as in words. That was why his next speech seemed to come out placidly enough. 'I doubt it's about time for us to quit.'

'I doubt it is.'

'I never meant to gang till I was carried,' Simon said, 'and then I doubt there'd still ha' been some o' me left. But I've seen the end o' things coming for a while back now. It seems kind o' meant, you being bothered wi' your eyes an' all.'

'Happen it is,' she said again, and sighed. Then she laughed, a slight laugh, but bitter and grim. 'It nobbut wanted that on top o' the rest!'

Simon threw her an uneasy glance.

'Nay, now, you mustn't get down about it, missis,' he said hastily. 'It waint do to get down. Doctor'll likely see his way to put you right. But we've had a terble poor time wi' it all,' he went on glumly, forgetting his own advice. 'Seems like as if we'd been overlooked by summat, you and me. 'Tisn't as if we'd made such a bad start at things, neither. We were both on us strong and willing when we was wed. It's like as if there'd been a curse o' some sort on the danged spot!'

'There's been a curse on the lot of us right enough!' Sarah said. 'Ay, and we don't need telling where it come from, neither!'

Again he looked at her with that uncomfortable air, though he took no notice of her bitter

speech. He knew only too well that haunted
corner of her mind. That sour, irreclaimable
pasture had been trodden in every inch.

'Ay, well, we're through on t'far side on't now,'
he said morosely. 'Sandholes can grind the soul
out o' some other poor body for the next forty
year! I never hear tell o' such a spot!' he went
on crossly, with that puzzled exasperation which
he always showed when discussing the marsh-
farm. 'It'd be summat to laugh at if only it didn't
make you dancin' mad! What, it's like as if even
slates had gitten a spite agen sticking to t'roof!
We've had t'tide in t'house more nor once, and
sure an' certain it'd be when we'd summat new
in the way o' gear. We'd a fire an' all, you'll think
on, and it took us a couple o' year getting to
rights agen. Burned out and drownded out—
why, it's right silly, that's what it is! As for t'land,
what, it fair swallers up lime an' slag and any
mak' o' manure, and does as lile or nowt as it can
for it in return. Nigh every crop we've had yet
was some sort of a let-down—that's if we'd
happen luck to get it at all! Kitchen garden's
near as bad; lile or nowt'll come up in't, nobbut
you set by it and hod its hand! Ay, and the stock,
now—if there was sickness about, sure an' certain
it'd fix on us. You'd nobbut just to hear tell o'
foot and mouth, or anthrax, or summat o' the
sort, an' it'd be showing at Sandholes inside a
week! Same wi' t'folk in t'house as wi' folk in
t'shuppon—fever, fluenzy, diphthery—the whole
doctor's bag o' tricks. Nay, there's summat
queer about t'spot, and that's Bible truth! We
should ha' made up our minds to get shot of it
long since, and tried our luck somewheres else.'

'We'd likely just ha' taken our luck along wi'
us,' Sarah said, 'and there was yon brass we'd
sunk in the spot—ay, and other folks' brass an'
all.' (Simon growled 'Ay, ay,' to this, but in
a reproachful tone, as if he thought it might well
have been left unsaid.) 'We were set enough on
Sandholes when we was wed, think on; and when
Geordie was running about as a bit of a lad.'

'Ay, and Jim.'

'Nay, then, I want nowt about Jim!'

'Ay, well, it's a bit since now,' Simon said
hastily, thinking that it seemed as long ago as
when there was firm land stretching from Ireland
to the marsh.

'Over forty year.'

'It's a bit since,' he said again, just as he said
equally of the creation of the world, or his own
boyhood, or the last time he was at Witham Show.

'Surely to goodness we were right enough then?
We shouldn't ha' said thank you for any other
spot. Nay, and we wouldn't ha' gone later on,
neither, if we'd gitten chanst. It would never ha'
done for Geordie to come back and find the old
folks quit.'

'Nay, nor for Jim——' he began again thought-
lessly, and bit it off. 'Ay, well, I doubt he'll
never come back now!'

'He's likely best where he is.' Sarah shut her
mouth with a hard snap. Once again she stared
straight in front of her over the horse's head,
staring and staring at the image which she had
set up.

A motor-horn challenged them presently from
behind, and Simon pulled aside without even
turning his head. He had never really grown

used to the cars and the stricter rule of the road.
He belonged to the days when the highway to
Witham saw a leisurely procession of farmers'
shandrydans, peat-carts, and carriers' carts with
curved hoods; with here and there a country
gentleman's pair of steppers flashing their way
through. He never took to the cars with their
raucous voices and trains of dust, their sudden
gusts of passage which sent his heart into his
mouth. His slack-reined driving forced him to
keep to the crown of the road, and only an always
forthcoming miracle got him out of the way in
time. He used to shrink a little when the cars
drew level, and the occupants turned their curious
heads. Somehow the whole occurrence had the
effect of a definite personal attack. Sometimes
he thought they laughed at the jolting trap, the
shabby old couple and the harness tied with
string. The rush of the cars seemed to bring a
crescendo of mocking voices and leave a trail of
diminishing mirth. But as a matter of fact he did
not often look at them when they looked at him.
There was nothing to link their hurrying world
with his.

This particular car, however, seemed an unusually long time in getting past. The horn
sounded again, and, muttering indignantly, he
pulled still farther into the hedge-side. He held
his breath for the usual disturbance and rush,
but they did not come. The car kept closely
behind him, but it did not pass. Round each
corner, as they reached it, he lost and then caught
again the subdued purring of the engine and the
soft slurring of the wheels. When they met anything, it fell farther back, so that at times he felt

sure that it must have stopped. Then he would
draw his breath, and drop into a walk, but almost
at once it would be at his back again. The note
of it grew to have a stealthy, stalking sound, as
of something that waited to spring upon its prey.

The strangeness of this proceeding began
suddenly to tell upon Simon's nerves. Lack of
interest had at first prevented him from turning
his head, but now it changed into sheer inability
to look behind. Soon he was in the grip of a panic
fear that the car at his back might not be a real
car, after all. He began to think that he had only
imagined the horn, the gentle note of the engine
and the soft sound of the wheels. Perhaps, now
that he was old, his ears were playing him false,
just as Sarah's eyes, so it seemed, were suddenly
playing her false. Presently he was sure, if he
turned, he would see nothing at all, or that,
instead of nothing at all, he would see a ghost.
Something that moved in another world would
be there, with spidery wheels and a body through
which he could see the fields; something that had
once belonged to life and gone out with a crash,
or was only just coming into it on the road. . . .

It was quite true that there was something
peculiar about the behaviour of the car. From its
number, it must have come from the county next
below, and it was splashed as if it had travelled
far and fast. During the last few miles, however,
it had done nothing but crawl. More than one
farmer had heard it behind him and wondered
why it took so long to pass, but it had never
dallied and dawdled so long before. Almost at
once it had gathered speed and slithered by, and
the man inside had turned with a friendly hail.

He was a stranger, so they said afterwards, with a puzzled air, but at the time they answered the hail as if he were one of themselves.

But Simon, at least, had no intention of hailing anybody just then. Indeed, he was fast losing both his sense and his self-control. He slapped the reins on the horse's back, making urgent, uncouth sounds, and doing his best to yank it into a sharper trot. It plunged forward with an air of surprise, so that the old folks bumped in their seats, knocked against each other and were jerked back. Presently it bundled itself into an aged gallop, while Simon clicked at it through his scanty teeth.

'Nay, now, master, what are you at!' Sarah protested, gripping the rail. 'We've no call to hurry ourselves, think on.'

'It's yon danged car!' Simon growled, feeling somehow as though he were galloping, too. He was quite sure now that a boggle was hot on his track, and the sweat stood on his brow as he slapped and lashed. Losing his nerve completely, he got to his feet with a shout, at the same time waving the car to pass ahead. It obeyed instantly, drawing level in a breath, and just for a breath slowing again as it reached his side. The hired driver was wearing a cheerful grin, but the man leaning out of the back of the car was perfectly grave. He was a big man, tanned, with steady grey-blue eyes, fixed on the old couple with an earnest gaze. Simon, however, would not have looked at him for gold, and after its momentary hesitation, the car shot on. The horse felt its master drop back again in his seat and subsided, panting, into its slowest crawl.

Sarah straightened her bonnet, and tugged at her mantle upon which Simon had collapsed. 'Whatever took you to act like yon?' she asked. 'There was nowt to put you about as I could see.'

'It was yon danged car!' Simon muttered again, but beginning already to feel rather ashamed. 'It give me the jumps, taking so long to get by. What, I got thinking after a bit it wasn't a motor-car at all! More like a hearse it seemed, when it ganged past—a gert, black hearse wi' nid-noddin' feathers on top. . . .' He let out a great sigh, mopping his face as if he would never stop. 'Danged if yon new strap baint gone and give out first thing!'

He climbed down, grumbling at the new strap which had gone back on him so soon, and began to add a fresh ornamentation to the mended gear. The horse stood with drooped head, emitting great breaths which shook and stirred the trap. Simon's hands trembled as he worked at his woolly knot, his eyes still full of that vision of sweeping plumes. Farther down the road the car had stopped again, but as soon as Simon had finished, it moved away. It went over the hill as if it indeed had wings—feathery, velvet-black and soft on the misty air. . . .

II

ANOTHER thing happened to them on the road to Witham, though it was even more trivial than the last. The first, perhaps, was meant for Simon—that face coming out of the void and trying to look him in the eyes. The other—a voice from the void—was a call to the woman with the failing sight. But to most people there come these

days of slight, blind, reasonless events. Something that is not so much memory as re-vision
reaches out of the past into the present; faint
foretellings shape themselves out of some far-off
hour. And then on the following morning there
is sun, and clear outlines and a blowing sky. The
firm circlet of To-Day is bound again shining and
hard about the narrow earth.

For a short time they seemed almost alone on
the processional road. No more cars passed them,
and only occasionally a bicycle or a trap. Simon
felt more than ever ashamed of himself as his
nerve steadied and his excitement cooled. He
had made a bonny fool of himself, he thought,
standing up and shouting as if he was cracked.
Witham would snap at the tale like a meaty bone,
and folk would be waiting to twit him when he
got in. It wasn't as if he were in the mood for a
joke, either, seeing how things were; he would
find it hard to take it as it was meant. And there
was one person at least to whom the tale would
be balm in Gilead for many a happy day. He
hoped fervently that it might not reach her
ears.

Sooner or later it would reach her, of course;
everything that made mock of them always did.
The most that could be hoped for was that they
would not meet her to-day, backed by her usual
sycophantic crowd. Sarah would never stand
any nonsense from her to-day, depressed as she
was by the trouble about her eyes. There would
be a scuffle between them, as sure as eggs were
eggs, and just when he wanted things smooth in
that quarter, too. He thought of giving her a
hint to be careful, and opened his mouth, and

then decided to keep off the subject, and shut it again.

Not that they ever *did* keep off it, as he knew perfectly well. Sooner or later it was on their lips, and certainly always after a day at market. They had discussed it so often from every possible point that they did not always know which of them it was that spoke. They had long since forgotten from which of their minds the bitter, perpetual speeches had first been born. Often they waked in the night to talk of the hated thing, and slept and wakened only to talk of it again. There was nothing good that they had which it had not poisoned at the source, and no sorrow but was made a double sorrow thereby. There was scarcely one of their memories that did not ache because of that constant sword-point in its heart.

It was on market-day each week that their fount of bitterness was continually refreshed. They kept up the old habit for more reasons than one, but most of all because of this thing which hurt and cramped their lives. It was like a vice of some sort which had long become an imperative need. Each week they came home with the iron fresh sunk in their souls, and each week they went again to look on the thing that they both loathed.

Now they were right away from the marsh and the sands, and would not see them until they returned, although from the moor and fell-land surrounding Witham it was always possible to see the bay. Indeed, in this part of the little county it was hard to get away from the knowledge of the sea; and even farther in, among the shouldering peaks, you had only to climb awhile to find the water almost within a throw. On days like this, however, even on the beach it was hard to tell which was water and which mist; and when at last the tide drew silently from beneath, those who looked at it from the hills could not tell whether it went or stayed.

Simon, looking drearily around, thought that the whole earth had a drowned appearance to-day. It reminded him of the marsh after it had been swamped by a flood, and the miserable land emerged soddenly as the sea drew back. Everything was so still, too, with the stillness of the dead or drugged. Only the mist moved steadily and of set purpose, though it was the purpose of a creature with shut eyes walking in its sleep.

Out of the low vapour softly roofing the fields a gull came flying slowly over their heads. First Simon saw the shadow of it huge upon the mist, and then it came swooping and circling until it hung above the road. Its long, pointed wings and drooping legs were magnified by the distorting air, and presently he could see the colour of its bill and the gleam of its expressionless eye. It moved in that lifeless atmosphere as a ship that has lost the wind moves still by its gathered momentum over a deadened sea; but when it came over the road it turned to follow the trap, instead of making away at an angle towards the west. Simon concluded that it must have lost its way in the mist, and was following them as sea-birds follow a boat, but presently he was reminded of the car in this leisurely gliding on their track. Like the car, too, it drew level at last, but this time he was not afraid. He looked

up at it, indeed, but without much interest,
watching its lone vagrancy with apathetic eyes.
It was silent at first as it circled and swooped,
looping its aimless, unnecessary curves, yet
always travelling on. It might have been a piece
of the wandering mist that had taken shape,
yet the sluggish, unbuoyant atmosphere seemed
scarcely to have sufficient strength to carry its
weight. So low it flew at last that it almost
brushed their faces and the horse's ears, and
in fancy he felt the touch of it damp and soft
against his cheek. And then, as it dropped for
the hundredth time, it suddenly spoke.

Sarah started violently when the cry broke
over her head, the harsh wailing cry that makes
all sands desolate and all moorland lone. She
lifted her face to search the curtained sky as well
as she could, but already the bird had left them
and mounted higher, as if called and turned to
another road. Each cry as it came was fainter
than the last, like the speech of a passing soul
ever farther off. There was about it something of
the majesty and terror of all irrevocable retreats,
of those who go forth unhesitatingly when sum-
moned, never to return. It left behind it the
same impulse to reach out passionate, yearning
arms, to cry aloud for the fainting answer that
would still go on long after the ear had ceased to
take it in.

Sarah sat with her face lifted to the last,
trembling and drawing short, uneven breaths.
Simon was silent until she had settled again, and
then—'It was nobbut a gull,' he said, at length.

She gave a deep sigh, and folded her hands
tightly before her in their black cotton gloves.

'We've plenty of 'em, I'm sure, down on t'marsh. I'm that used to them, I never hear their noise.'

She turned her head slightly towards him, as if in a vain attempt to see his face.

'Ay, but it was *that like*,' she answered in a suppressed tone. 'Eh, man, but it was terble like!'

He gave a grunt by way of reply, knowing well enough what she meant, but knowing also that there was nothing to say. It was not true, of course, that he never heard the gulls. He heard them always, and behind them the voice that called across the years. But they had long since ceased to talk about it or to take the voice of the present for the voice of the past. Sometimes, indeed, when the cry came at the window on a stormy night, they started and looked at each other, and then looked away. But it was not often that they were deceived, as Sarah had been, to-day. Even now, he felt sure, she was straining after the voice, that would never cease crying until it reached the tide.

They were passed again before they reached the town, but this time it was by the cheerful rap of hoofs. It caught them as they creaked their way up the last hill—the smart going of a good horse that even on the smothered highway managed to ring sharp. A whip was waved as the dog-cart dashed by, and the driver turned back to give them a smile. She was Fleming's motherless daughter from the Ship Inn across the sands, and Simon and Sarah had known her all her life. All her life she had lived looking out across the bay, and half her life looking a thousand miles beyond.

Simon threw up his hand to her with an answering smile, a sudden sweetness changing his whole face. Even Sarah relaxed when she knew who it was, and both of them brightened for a little while. They were fond of May, a good girl who did not change, and who never made light of those whom Fate was counting out. She had always had the power to strengthen their hold on life, to blow their dying courage into a flame. There was a serene yet pulsing strength about her that had the soothing stimulus of a summer tide. Sarah had been jealous of her when she was young, and had fended her off, but May had long since found her patient way to her heart. Now she stood to both the old people as their one firm link with the past, and as such she was more precious to them than rubies and dearer than bright gold.

'A good lass!' Simon observed, with the smile still present on his lips.

'Ay.'

'I've always thought a deal o' May.'

'Ay, an' me.'

'Geordie an' all,' he added, with a faintly mischievous air.

Sarah did not speak.

'An' Jim——'

'Nay, then, I want nowt about Jim!'

Simon drew the lash gently along the horse's back.

'I hear Fleming's been none so well lately,' he resumed, as they rumbled into Witham. 'We mun think on to ax. Happen I could slip across to t' "Ship" after we've gitten back. Tide's about six, isn't it? I could happen do it.'

'Fleming's nobbut going the same road as t'rest on us,' Sarah said. 'He'll be glad to see you, though, like enough. But it'll be dark soon, think on, wi' all this fog.'

'There's summat queer about t'weather,' Simon said broodingly, knitting his brows. 'Tides is fairish big, and yet it's terble whyet. Happen we'll have a change o' some sort afore so long.'

'I've noticed it's often whyet afore a big change. Seems like as if it knew what was coming afore it was on t'road.'

'Ay, but it's different, some way. . . . It's more nor that. There's a blind look about things, seems to me.'

'Blind weather for blind folk!' Sarah put in, with a grim laugh. Simon grunted a protest, but she took no notice. 'I never thought as I should be blind,' she went on, almost as if to herself. 'I've always been terble sharp wi' my eyes; likely that's why I've managed to wear 'em out. And I've always been terble feared o' folks as couldn't see. There's no telling what blind weather and a blind body's brain may breed. . . . Ay, well, likely I'll know a bit more about they sort o' things now. . . .'

III

ALL old and historical towns seem older and richer in meaning on some days than they do on others. But the old and the rich days are also the most aloof. The towns withdraw, as it were, to ponder on their past. By some magic of their own they eliminate all the latest features, such as a library, a garage, or a new town hall, and show you nothing but winding alleys filled with leaning

walls and mossy roofs. The eye finds for itself
with ease things which it has seen for a lifetime
and yet never seen—carved stone dates, colour-
washed houses jutting out over worn pillars, grey,
mullioned houses tucked away between the
shops. The old pigments and figures stand out
strangely on the well-known signs, and the old
names of the inns make a new music in the ear.
The mother-church by the river seems bowed to
the earth with the weight of the prayers that cling
to her arched roof. The flags in the chancel seem
more fragile than they did last week. The whole
spirit of the town sinks, as the eyelids of the old
sink on a twilit afternoon.

Witham wore this air of detachment when
Simon and Sarah came to it to-day, as if it held
itself apart from one of the busiest spectacles
of the year. The long main street, rising and
dipping, but otherwise running as if on a terrace
cut in the side of the hill, was strung from end to
end with the scattered units of the road. The
ambling traffic blocked and dislocated itself with
the automatic ease of a body of folk who are
all acquainted with each other's ways. Groups
clustered on the pavements, deep in talk, and
overflowed carelessly into the street. Horses'
heads came up over their shoulders and car
wheels against their knees, without disturbing
either their conversation or their nerves. Sheep-
dogs hung closely at their masters' heels, or
slipped with a cocked eye between the hoofs.
The shops were full, but those who wandered
outside to wait could always find a friend to fill
their time. Simon's personal cronies jerked their
heads at him as he passed, and the busy matrons

nodded a greeting as they hurried in front of the horse's nose.

He made as if to draw up at the house of a well-known doctor in the town, but Sarah stopped him before he reached the kerb. 'Nay, nay,' she said nervously, 'it'll likely bide. I don't know as I'm that fain to hear what he's got to say. Anyway, I'd a deal sooner get my marketing done first.'

So instead of stopping they went straight to the inn where they had put up on market-day for the last forty years, and where Simon's father had put up before Simon was born. Turning suddenly across the pavement through a narrow entry, they plunged sharply downhill into a sloping yard. The back premises of old houses shut it in on every side, lifting their top windows for a glimpse of the near moor. The inn itself, small and dark, with winding staircases and innumerable doors, had also this sudden vision of a lone, high world against the sky.

An ancient ostler came to help Simon with the horse, while Sarah waited on the sloping stones. The steep yard was full of traps, pushed under sheds or left in the open with their shafts against the ground. Fleming's dog-cart was there, with its neat body and light wheels; but May was already gone on her business in the town. Simon had an affection for a particular spot of his own, and it always put him about to find it filled. It was taken this morning, he found, though not by May. May would never have played him a trick like that. It was a car that was standing smugly in Simon's place, with a doubled-up driver busy about its wheels. Cars were always intruders in the cobbled old yard, but it was a personal insult to find one in his 'spot.' He went and talked to the driver about it in rising tones, and the driver stood on his head and made biting comments between his feet. A man came to one of the inn windows while the scene was on, and listened attentively to the feast of reason and the flow of soul.

Sarah looked rather white and shaky by the time Simon returned, thinking of something new to say to the very last. He left the newest and best unsaid, however, when he saw her face.

'You'd best set down for a bit,' he observed, leading her anxiously towards the inn. 'You're fretting yourself about seeing doctor, that's what it is. You'd ha' done better to call as we come in.'

But Sarah insisted that she was not troubling about the doctor in the least. She had been right as a bobbin, she said, and then she had suddenly come over all queer. 'Happen it's standing that long while you and morter-man sauced each other about car!' she added, with shaky spirit. 'You made a terble song about it, I'm sure. Trap'll do well enough where it is.'

'I can't abide they morter-folk!' Simon muttered, crestfallen but still vexed. 'But never mind about yon. Gang in and set you down. If I happen across May, I'll tell her to look you up.'

A door opened at the end of the dark passage, showing a warm parlour with flowers and crimson blinds. The stout landlady came swimming towards them, speaking as she swam, so that the vibrations of her welcoming voice reached them first like oncoming waves. Another door opened in the wall on the right, and a man looked out from the dim corner behind.

'That you, Mrs. Thornthet? What?—not so well? Nay, now, it'll never do to start market-day feeling badly, I'm sure! Come along in and rest yourself by t'fire, and a cup of tea'll happen set you right.'

Sarah, shaken and faint, and longing to sit down, yet hesitated as if afraid to step inside. It seemed to her, as she paused, that there was some ordeal in front of her which she could not face. Her heart beat and her throat was dry, and though she longed to go in, she was unable to stir. The man inside saw her against a background of misty yard, a white face and homely figure dressed in threadbare black. Once or twice his gaze left her to dwell on Simon, but it was always to the more dramatic figure that it returned. There was a current in the passage, full and sweeping like the wind that went before the still, small Voice of God. Sarah was caught by it, urged forward, filled with it with each breath. But even as she lifted her foot she heard a woman's voice in the room beyond.

'We've Mrs. Will here an' all,' the landlady called, as she swam away. 'She'll see to you if there's anything you want, I'm sure.'

She might just as well have slammed and locked the door in the old folks' teeth. At once they made a simultaneous movement of recoil, stiffening themselves as if against attack. The spirit in the passage died down, leaving it filled to the ceiling with that heavy, chattering voice. Sarah was well away from the doorstep before she opened her mouth

'Nay, I don't know as I won't go right on, thank ye, Mrs. Bond. I'm feeling a deal better already—I am that. If I set down, I'll likely not feel like getting up again, and I've a deal to see to in t'town.'

Mrs. Bond swam back, concerned and surprised, but Sarah was already well across the yard. Simon, when appealed to, said nothing but, 'Nay, I reckon she'll do,' and seemed equally bent upon getting himself away. They retreated hurriedly through the arch that led to the street, leaving Mrs. Bond to say, 'Well, I never, now!' to the empty air. The man's face came back to the window as they went, looking after this sudden retirement with a troubled frown.

The driver was still working at his car when he found his passenger suddenly at his side. He was a queer customer, he thought to himself, looking up at the moody expression on his handsome face. He had behaved like a boy on their early morning ride, continually stopping the car, and then hustling it on again. He had sung and whistled and shouted at people on the road, laughed without any apparent reason, and dug the unfortunate driver in the back. He was clean off it, the man thought, grinning and vexed by turn, and wondering when and where the expedition would end. People as lively as that at blush of dawn were simply asking for slaps before the sun was down. He had steadied a trifle when they reached the Witham road, but the queerest thing of all that he did was that checking behind the traps. The driver was sure he was cracked by the time they got to the town, and he was surer than ever when he came out now and told him to move the car. He might have refused if his fare had not been so big and broad, and if he had not already shown himself generous on the road. As it was, he found himself, after a moment of sulky surprise, helping to push the trap into the disputed place. He still wore his injured expression when he went back to his job, but it was wasted on his employer, who never looked his way. Instead, he was standing and staring at Simon's crazy rig, and he smiled as he stared, but it was not a happy smile. Presently he, too, made his way to the arch, and disappeared into the crowded street.

The old folks had seemed in a terrible hurry to be gone, but, as a matter of fact, they halted as soon as they got outside. 'I couldn't ha' gone in there whatever,' Sarah said, in an apologetic tone, and Simon nodded, looking anxiously up and down.

'If I could nobbut catch a sight o' May,' he muttered worriedly, searching the crowd. 'May'd see to you right off, and get you a snack o' summat an' all. I've Mr. Dent to see about chucking t'farm, and I've a two-three other things to do as well.'

But instead of May, who was nowhere to be seen, a man came shyly towards them from a neighbouring group. He was like Simon to look at, only younger and better clad, showing none of the other's signs of trouble and hard toil. His voice was like Simon's, too, when Simon was at his best, but Sarah stiffened when she heard him speak.

'You'll not ha' seen Fleming's lass?' Simon asked, devouring the street, and Will swung about at once to cast his own glance over the press.

'She was by, a minute since,' he said thoughtfully. 'She can't ha' gone far. . . .' He hunted a moment longer, and turned shyly back. 'Likely you'll give us a call at Blindbeck this afternoon?'

Sarah said nothing in reply to the invitation, but Simon gave a nod.

'I could do wi' a word wi' you, Will, if you're not throng. It's about time we were thinking o' making a change. Sarah's bothered wi' her eyes.'

'Nay, now, that's bad news, to be sure.' Will was genuinely concerned. He glanced at Sarah kindly, though with a diffident air. 'Happen a pair o' glasses'll fix you,' he said, in his gentle tones. There was a pause, and then he jerked his head towards the arch that led to the inn. 'I left my missis behind there, talking to Mrs. Bond. If you're thinking o' seeing t'doctor, you'd best have a woman to come along.'

'I meant to ax May,' Simon said hurriedly, praying for May to spring out of the ground, and, as if by way of reply, she came out of a shop on the far side. He plunged forward, waving and calling her name, and she stopped, smiling, as he caught her by the arm. She was grave at once, however, when she heard what he had to say, and her eyes rested on Sarah with a troubled look. She gave a nod of comprehension when he pointed towards the arch, and, without waiting to hear more, crossed over to Sarah's side. By the time the stranger appeared, the women had vanished down the street, while the brothers were making their way to the market square. This was the second time that the Thornthwaites had fled at the sound of a name, and this time, as it happened, May was sent speeding away, too.

IV

MAY, however, was only thinking of how she could be of use, and was very cheery and pleasant all along the street. Already she had come across one or two pieces of news, and laughed about them to Sarah until Sarah was laughing, too. Once or twice they met somebody who had something else to tell, and they stood on the pavement together and thrashed the matter out. May's laugh sounded young and gay, and a girlish colour came into her cheeks. The old figure beside her seemed to draw vitality from her generous warmth, her brave air which made an adventure of every commonplace of life. Sarah even rose to a joke or two on her own account, and was wonderfully heartened when they got to the doctor's house. She would not hear of having a cup of tea or even a rest. Time enough for such things, she said with spirit, when they were through.

She had both of them, however, at the doctor's, because he would not let her go away without. May took her into the dining-room by his orders, and found her an easy chair beside the fire. A parlourmaid brought a tray, and Sarah drank her tea cheerfully enough, soothed by the comfort and quiet and the presence of some sweet-smelling flower. The doctor had been kindness itself, and had felt a little depressed when he sent the women away. He did not know that the last thing that was in their minds as they sat by the fire was the terrible fact that Sarah was going blind.

They spoke of it, indeed, but only casually, as it were, before passing on to the greater thing at its back. Sarah's sense of courtesy forced her at least to give the doctor a pat on the head.

'Ay, he was right kind,' she said in a matter-of-fact tone, 'and I will say this for him that he seemed to know his job. I've had my doubts for a while there was summat badly wrong. I don't know as it's news to me, after all. As for yon operation he says might do summat for me, I doubt I'm over old. We've no brass for notions o' that sort, neither, come to that.'

'There's hospitals,' May said—'homes and suchlike where they take you free. Plenty of folk go to 'em, even at your age, and they'd see to you well enough, I'm sure.'

'Ay, doctor said that an' all,' Sarah assented, though in an uninterested tone. 'But I'd only take badly to they sort o' spots now,' she added, sipping her tea. 'I'd be marching out agen, likely, as soon as ever I'd set my foot inside of the door.'

'They say folks settle wonderfully when they've made up their minds. It's worth a bit of trouble, if they put you right.'

'Happen,' Sarah said casually, and withdrew it at once. 'I don't know as it is.'

'You're down, that's what it is. You'll feel better after a bit.'

'I don't know as I shall.'

'You'll feel different about it in a day or two. You'd come through it right as a bobbin. You've pluck enough for ten.'

'Ay, well, I can't settle it one way or t'other,' Sarah said stubbornly, turning a deaf ear. 'Things is a bit ham-sam just now,' she added evasively, fiddling with her cup, and wondering why she

could not bring herself to announce that they
were leaving the farm. But as long as they did not
speak of it, it was just as if nothing had happened,
as though the words which had framed the
decision had never been said. And yet at that
very moment Simon was probably telling Will
and Mr. Dent, and the news would be racing
its way round Witham until it came to Eliza's
ear. . . .

'We'll work it some way,' May urged, not
knowing of the big pause that had come into
Sarah's life. 'You may have to get a word put
in for you, but that's easy done. I'll see the
Squire and Mrs. Wilson and maybe a few more,
and it'll be all fixed up without you putting
yourself about.'

'You're right kind, you are that.'

'It's worth it,' May said again.

'Ay . . . I don't know . . .' Sarah answered her
absently, and then sat up straight. 'It'd ha' been
worth it once,' she broke out suddenly, as if
letting herself go. 'There was a time when I'd a
deal sooner ha' been dead than blind, but it
don't matter much now. There's not that much
left as I care to look at, I'm sure. It's the eyes
make the heart sore more nor half the time. But
I'd ha' felt badly about it if Geordie was coming
back, and I couldn't ha' framed to see his face.'

May said—'It's best not to think of such
things,' as cheerfully as she could, but her own
face clouded as she spoke, and suddenly she
looked old. Here was the old trouble, if the
doctor had known, that was still big enough to
make the new one seem almost small. Blindness
was not so dreadful a thing to these two women,

who had both of them lost the light of their eyes so long before. Long ago they had known what it was to rise and see no shine in the day, no blue in the sea for May who had lost her lover, no sun in the sky for Sarah without her child.

It was twenty years now since Geordie had gone away, clearing out overseas as casually as if into the next field. Eliza's eldest from Blindbeck had gone as well, as like him in face and voice as if hatched in the same nest. They were too lively, too restless for the calm machinery of English country life, and when the call came from over the ocean they had vanished in a night. Canada, which has so many links with Westmorland now, seemed farther away then than the world beyond the grave. Death at least left you with bones in a green yard and a stone with a graven name, but Canada made you childless, and there was no sign of your grief beneath the church's wall. Geordie had written, indeed, from time to time, but though the letters were light enough on the top, there was heartache underneath. He was a failure there, they gathered, after a while, just as they were failures here; as if the curse of the Sandholes luck had followed even across the sea. Jim was a failure, too, as far as they knew, though their impression of Jim's doings was always vague. His very name on the page seemed to have the trick of dissolving itself in invisible ink, and his own letters were never answered and barely even read. He had been fond of his aunt, but Sarah had given him only the scantiest tolerance in return. Sarah, indeed, would not have cared if Jim had been burning in everlasting fire. . . .

'We'd a letter from Geordie a month back,' she said suddenly, after the pause, 'begging the loan of a pound o' two to fetch him home.'

May started a little, and the colour came back to her cheek. It was a long time now since anything fresh about Geordie had come her way. Once she had been in the habit of going to Sandholes for news, asking for it by indirect methods of which she was still rather ashamed. Sarah had been jealous of her in those days and grudged her every word; and since she had stopped being jealous there had been next to nothing to grudge. . . .

'Ay, he axed for his fare, but we hadn't got it to send. I don't know as we want him, neither, if he can't shape better than that.'

May felt her heart shake as she leaned forward, clasping her hands.

'I've a bit put by I could spare,' she began, with a thrill in her voice. 'It could go from you, Mrs. Thornthet—he need never know. You've only to say the word, and you can have it when you want.'

A twinge of the ancient jealousy caught suddenly at Sarah's heart. With difficulty she remembered May's kindness and the long bond of the years.

'I'll not spend any lass's savings on *my* lad!' she answered roughly, and then softened again. 'Nay, May, my girl, you mean well enough, but it wain't do. Losh save us! Hasn't he done badly enough by you, as it is?' she added grimly. 'You should ha' been wed this many a long year, instead o' hanging on for the likes o' him!'

'I doubt I'd never have married in any case,'

May said. 'I don't know as I'd ever have made up my mind to leave my dad.'

'You'd ha' wed right enough but for Geordie —dad or no dad!' Sarah scoffed. 'You're the sort as is meant to be wed, from the start. Nay, he's spoilt your life, and no doubt about it, but there's no sense in lossing the can because you've gone and spilt the milk. Say you sent him the brass, and he come back without a cent, what'd be the end o' the business then? You'd wed him, I'll be bound—for pity, if for nowt else. Your father'll likely leave you a nice bit, and you'd get along on that, but who's to say how Geordie'd frame after all these years? Happen he's lost the habit o' work by now, and it'll be a deal more likely than not if he's taken to drink.'

'Geordie wasn't that sort.' May shook her head. 'He'll not have taken to drink, not he!'

'Folks change out of all knowledge—ay, and inside as well as out.'

'Not if they're made right,' May said stubbornly, 'and Geordie was all right. He was a daft mafflin, I'll give you that, always playing jokes and the like, but it was just the life in him— nowt else. He was a fine lad then, in spite of it all, and I don't mind swearing that he's a fine man now.'

'Ay,' Sarah said slowly, 'fine enough, to be sure! A fine lad to leave his folks for t'far side o' the world wi' never a word! A fine man as can't look to himself at forty, let alone give his father and mother a bit o' help! . . . Nay, my lass, don't you talk to me!' she finished brusquely. 'We've thought a deal o' Geordie, me and Simon and you, but I reckon he's nowt to crack on, all the same!'

'You'd think different when he was back,' May pleaded—'I'm sure you would. And you needn't fret about me if that's all there is in the road. I made up my mind long since as I shouldn't wed. But I'd be rarely glad, all the same, to have had a hand in fetching him home.'

'You're real good, as I said, but it's over late.' She paused a moment and then went on again. 'Letter went a couple o' week ago.'

The tears came into May's eyes.

'You don't mean as you said him no? Eh, Mrs. Thornthet, but I'm sorry to hear that!'

'Yon sort o' thing's best answered right off.'

For a moment or two May put her hand to her face. 'Eh, but what a pity!' she murmured, after a while. 'What does it matter whose brass fetches him home?'

'It matters to me.'

'It matters a deal more that you're breaking your heart——'

'Nay, then, I'm not! ... Ay, well, then, what if I be?'

'Let me get the brass right off!' May said, in a coaxing tone. 'Let me—do now! Send it to him to-day.'

'Nay.'

'You've got it into your head he's different, but I'll swear you're wrong! Different in looks, maybe, but he'll be none the worse for that. He always framed to be a fine figure of a man when he was set. You'd be as throng wi' him as a clockie hen wi' a pot egg.'

Sarah snorted scorn, but her face softened a little.

'He's forty, but I'll be bound he hasn't changed.

I'll be bound he's nobbut the same merry lad inside.'

'Happen none the better for that.'

'Geordie isn't the sort as grows old—Geordie an' Jim——'

'Nay, then, I want nowt about Jim!' Sarah flared, and the other laughed.

'It's hard to think of 'em apart even now— they were that like. Why, I've mixed 'em myself, over and over again, and fine fun it was for them, to be sure!'

'*I* never mixed 'em!' Sarah snapped, with a blind glare. 'I never see a scrap o' likeness myself.'

'Why, the whole countryside couldn't tell 'em apart—school-folk an' all! 'Twasn't only their faces was like; 'twas their voices, too.'

'Hold your whisht!'

'You'll remember yon calls they had, Geordie an' Jim——'

'Whisht, I tell ye!' There was something scared as well as angry in Sarah's tone, and May was hushed into silence in spite of herself. 'Jim was sweet on you, too,' the old woman went on surlily, after a pause. 'If there wasn't that much to choose between 'em, why didn't you choose *him*?'

'There was all the world to choose between them, when it come to it,' May said smiling, but with tears in her voice. 'Once Geordie'd kissed me, I never mixed 'em up again!'

The rough colour came suddenly into Sarah's face. She tried to turn it away, with the pathetic helplessness of the blind who cannot tell what others may be reading there in spite of their will.

May, however, was looking away from her into the past.

'Not but what Jim was a rare good sort,' she was saying, with the tenderness of a woman towards a lover who once might have been and just was not. 'Eh, and how fond he was of you, Mrs. Thornthet!' she added, turning again. 'No lad could ha' thought more of his own mother than he did of you.'

'I wanted nowt wi' his fondness,' Sarah said in a hard tone. 'And I want no mewling about him now, as I said afore!'

'Ay, you told him off terrible, poor lad, but he was that set on you he didn't mind. He used to fetch you fairings and suchlike, didn't he—same as Geordie did? It was never his mother he fetched 'em for; 'twas always you.'

'Eliza never had no need o' fairings, wi' all she had at her back!' Sarah stood up sharply and began to grope about for her mantle and gloves. 'You're bringing things back just to coax me about yon brass!' she added, as May came forward to help. . . . 'Your father's none so well, I'm sorry to hear?'

'He hasn't been himself for a while now, and he's getting worse. I doubt he's going down the hill sharp-like, poor old chap!'

'Ay, well, our time comes to us all, and we wouldn't wish for owt else. But it'll be rare an' lonely for you wi'out him, all the same.'

'I'm used to being alone, though I can't say it's very grand. . . . You'll have to let me come and see to you and Mr. Thornthet,' she added, with a cheerful laugh.

'We're over old for the likes o' you. You want

friends of your own age to keep you lively-like.'

'I'm not so young myself, if it comes to that,' May said. 'And I don't know as I ever had a real friend, barring Geordie an' Jim.'

'That's enough o' the two on 'em!' Sarah snarled, as they went out. 'Geordie's been a bonny friend to you, anyway—he has that! We'd best be getting about our business. Talking o' things as is dead and gone won't make us any more lish.'

'Simon'll be bothered about my eyes,' she said presently, as they turned towards the shops. 'It's a deal worse having to tell him than to put up wi' it myself.'

'Happen you'd like me to tell him for you?' May suggested, but Sarah shook her head.

'Nay, you'd do it right enough, I'm sure,' she said kindly, 'but it'd come best from me. You've enough o' your own to fash you, wi'out that. Married folk mun do their own telling over things like yon. . . .'

V

BUT though Sarah had held to the telling of Simon, she seemed in no hurry to break the dismal news. All morning she clung to May, as if they drew together as a matter of course, and May was glad to have her, not only because she was old and needed help, but because of the tie between them which had never been loosed. It was true that they had seen little of each other of late years, but it had only needed the talk in the doctor's house to draw them together again. The dwelling upon a lost hope may sometimes make the impossible possible and the dead live, if only

for a space. The two of them had recreated
Geordie in the quiet room, so that his mother had
seen him plain before her darkened eyes, and his
sweetheart had felt his kisses on her lips.

So all morning they stayed together, even
though they did not speak of him again, because
while they were together the glamour persisted
and the dream remained. Just as one name had
robbed them, that day, though they did not know
it, so another name sweetened everything for
them, and for a little space made them rich.
Things might so easily have been as they wished
that it seemed as if even now just a little determination might twist them into shape. In the
ordinary course of events, and with ever such an
ordinary share of luck, Geordie and May should
have been married long ago, with a home of their
own to offer the old folk at the last. Even now,
so it seemed, Geordie might be somewhere in the
street, in the midst of that crowd of healthy youth,
sturdy manhood and wiry age. Instinctively, as
they came out of each shop, they looked to find
him the centre of some chaffing group, the
laughing, handsome, witty centre, as he had
always been. He would break away when he saw
them to ask his old mother how she did, and
suddenly the greatest and best of all happenings
would have happened, and they would have
heard the miracle of his speech. . . .

This was the spell they wove for each other,
making the day brighter and the world kinder,
and helping them to laugh at things which otherwise would have been too light to stir their hearts.
Sarah's shopping was dull and soon finished, but
May had an exciting list, and seemed constantly

in need of help. The old woman actually enjoyed herself as she peered at stockings and linen buttons, and nipped longcloth and serge between her finger and thumb. It might have been wedding-gear they were after, she told May, with a grim chuckle, and May laughed and sighed, thinking of a bottom drawer at home that had been locked for many years. The salesman laughed, too, and asked Sarah which of them it was that was thinking of getting wed, and Sarah, with all her arduous married life behind her, was yet as pleased as a young girl. She was a shrewd marketer, even now, in spite of her sight, especially in the food-shops, where one nose can often be quite as useful as a pair of eyes; while, as for pots and pans, she knew them as a hen knows her chickens and a shepherd his sheep.

They had many a chat over a counter, making and receiving enquiries about friends, opening their mouths at any lively piece of news, and pursing them sympathetically when there was trouble around the door. In the low shops with the new windows in their old walls and new slates on their bowed roofs, little, low doorways stooping for their heads, little, worn doorsteps watching for their feet, they heard many a hint of the romance of evolving or changing trade, many a precious historic touch that would never find its way into print. You cannot put your ear to the past anywhere but in the old places where men are born to their trades, where they know the customer's pedigree as the customer knows theirs, and where everybody has time for the human as well as the commercial exchange. Only there can you learn in the space of an hour

wonderful things about drapery and furniture
and hardware and tea, and feel the glamour of
the whole budding and fruit-bearing earth come
into the florist's, and the atmosphere of old
posting-inns into the pot-shop with the clink of
glass. And no man who is born to his trade is
ever a cobbler who may not look beyond his last.
The potman will tell you where to order a stylish
suit of clothes, and the florist instruct you how to
smoke a ham. And every one of them will tell you,
with or without their knowing it, what they have
learned of human nature and the hope of eternity
in their quiet little town, and with what eyes
they have looked abroad upon the world.

All that morning the tides of life swept against
Sarah and her friend as they went about the streets
—tides of humanity and sympathy, memory and
custom—all the currents that move in the air and
the blood and the brain when a hand is shaken,
or a friendly voice is heard. It was life at its
fullest, as it is known to the northern farmer and
his kind, the public recognition in a given place
of the great and intimate system of which he is
a part. The dumb beasts had their place in it,
too—perhaps the chief place—and though only
the wise dogs and the cobby, half-clipped horses
were there in the flesh, the all-absorbing stock
was never absent from the mind. Into every
conversation before so long some grand bull-calf
or pedigree shearling was sure to push its way.
Moving among the warm human tides was like
moving in a flood, while, overhead, low almost
as the roofs, the mist drifted and the sky drooped.
Seven miles away, the sands lay bare as a hand, as
if never in any æon of time would the sea return.

Sarah and May had their dinner together in a café overlooking one of the steep streets, and, choosing a table by one of the windows, so that they could look out, spread their parcels about them, and discussed their bargains and their mistakes. They were still happy, as happiness went for them in those days, because of the miracle that seemed always possible down in the street. Folks in plenty were coming and going on the narrow stair, and as each head rose above the floor of the room in which they sat, they felt a thrill of anticipation that was yet too slight to bring disappointment in its train. May, perhaps, was slightly puzzled by the persistence of the feeling in the air, but Sarah was well-used, like all who are old, to the strange reality of these glamour-days that are fashioned from the past.

They had their heads together over a new-fangled floor-cloth when the ubiquitous stranger came quietly up the stairs; and they were so absorbed and Sarah was so exuberant in her wrath, that he had time to look about him before the final word was said. There was no room for him, he saw, except at the table where they sat, and, presently, though rather uncertainly, he advanced a foot. If they had looked at him, he would have gone forward at once, but when they lifted their eyes it was only to turn them towards the window and the street. The little action seemed somehow to shut him out, and, drawing back almost guiltily, he found a seat for himself in the adjoining room. May looked round as he did so, just as though somebody had called, and stared intently at the place where he had been. He could still see them, however, from where he sat, and he noticed many things about them as he watched. He noticed, for instance, how strong and capable May looked, like a woman who had long since taken her life in her hands and ruled it well. He noticed her good clothes and Sarah's shabby ones, and that the multitudinous parcels were most of them May's. He noticed the shake which time, in spite of her, had put into Sarah's hands, and was puzzled by the groping manner in which she used her fork. He noticed that the two of them ate little and that without much heart, and that always they turned their faces towards the street. And finally he noticed how Sarah, in the midst of her talk, went suddenly rigid as a woman came into the room.

She was a big woman over sixty years of age, with smooth, high-coloured cheeks and thick dark hair that was still a long way from turning white. Her face said plainly that she had had a full, comfortable, healthy life, with plenty to interest her and little to fret. Her brown eyes, which had been beautiful in youth, had kept their expression of self-satisfaction wholly undisturbed. She looked, indeed, what she was, the mother of a big family, the mistress of a good-class farm, and the wife of a man whose banking account had long since ceased to keep him awake at night. She wore a black hat and a black plush coat, and round her shoulders was a big fur wrap. In a kid-gloved hand she carried a muff and a silver-mounted bag, and May, looking down, saw patent-toed boots showing beneath her neat, black skirt. Sarah was sure of them, too, though she could not see them. It was not with her

physical eye that she looked at Eliza of Blindbeck, Simon's brother's wife.

She, too, had paused in the doorway, looking
for a place, but as soon as she saw the two in the
window, she advanced at once. As she passed,
she spoke to several people in a noisy, hearty
voice, that seemed to have a blustering quality
somewhere at its back. By the time she had
reached Sarah's table, and come to a stop, the
man in the other room noticed that Sarah had
suddenly grown small. . . .

'Eh, now, if I haven't been seeking you all over
the shop!' Eliza exclaimed. 'Will had it you
wanted me most particular, so I've been looking
out. I couldn't find you, though, whatever I did.
I never see folks so set on keeping out of the road!'

Sarah still continued to look as though she had
shrunk. Even her voice seemed to have grown
less. It sounded far off and rather prim.

'Nay, I don't know as I did, thank ye,' was all
she said. 'Will mun ha' gitten hold o' the wrong
end o' the stick.'

Eliza looked at her with the little smile which
the sight of Sarah always brought to her lips. She
pulled a chair towards her and collapsed into it
without waiting to be asked.

'Ay, well, that's queer, to be sure! Will's no
more muddled than most on market-day, as a
rule. I made sure you were wanting me right off
the reel, from what he said.'

May explained nervously that she had come to
Sarah's assistance instead. Eliza always made
her nervous, because she never seemed to know
she was in the room. 'There wasn't that much
to do,' she finished hurriedly, stumbling over her

words. 'It's a pity Mr. Thornthwaite set you looking her up.'

'Nay, I don't know. . . . I'd have been glad to do anything, I'm sure!' Eliza spoke in her heartiest tones, so that everybody could hear. 'Nobody can say I'm one as can't be bothered to lend a hand. I reckon me and Will have done as much in that line as most.' She looked at Sarah again, the smile growing on her lips. . . . 'You'll not mind me sitting down with you, I suppose?'

'We're through, thank ye. We're just off.' Sarah pushed her plate from her, and began to fumble shakily for the thread gloves. May looked across at her with a troubled glance, and gathered the parcels together, ready to move. Eliza, however, had no intention of allowing them to escape so soon.

'You're surely not thinking o' stirring yet!' she exclaimed, in a hurt tone. 'What, we've barely as much as passed the time o' day! You'll not grudge me a word or two after all my trouble, and me that throng wi' shopping I didn't know where to turn. Will was as full of nods and becks as a row o' poppies in a wind, and I've been fair aching ever since to know what he could be at.'

She turned in her seat to call a waitress, and ordered a substantial meal; after which, throwing back her fur, she leaned her arms on the table, and resumed her smile. Everybody in the place knew what Eliza Thornthwaite was having for her dinner, and here and there they were saying to each other, 'They do themselves rarely at Blindbeck. . . . There's a deal o' brass to Blindbeck . . . ay, Blindbeck's plenty o' brass!' Eliza knew what they were saying, of course, and felt unctuously pleased; but May's heart swelled as she looked at Sarah's scanty, unfinished repast and the thin thread gloves that she was smoothing over her wrists. Eliza had taken off her own gloves by now, showing thick fingers and short nails. They were trapped in the alcove as long as she sat the table-end, because of her big, over-flowing figure which shut the two of them in. They would have to push their way past her if they wanted to get out, and Sarah would never as much as touch her with the end of a ten-foot pole.

'I'd ha' done what I could, I'm sure,' Eliza was busy telling them again. 'I'd never say no to folks as can't help themselves. But there—I needn't ha' bothered about it—you're as right as rain. Will had it you were off to t'doctor's, but I made sure he was wrong. I haven't seen you looking so well for a month o' Sundays, and that's the truth.'

She raised herself as the waitress set a steaming plate in front of her, and stared at it critically.

'Eh, well, you've not that much to bother you, have you?' she added kindly, setting to work— 'nobbut Simon to see to, and just that bit of a spot? 'Tisn't the same for you as it is for me, with that great place of our'n on my hands, and the house fair crowded out.'

Sarah did not speak, but she saw, as she was intended to see, a picture of the good farm where Mrs. Will reigned supreme, of her sons and daughters and their friends, and her hired lasses and lads; and after that another picture of her own empty home, where no youthful steps sounded along the floors, and no vibrant young voices rang against the roof. The pictures hurt her, as they were meant to do, as well as the cheerful comment upon her looks. Eliza always assumed that you were as strong as a horse, even if you lay on your death-bed at her feet.

'I never heard tell you were badly,' she persisted, fixing her eyes on Sarah's face, which looked like parchment against the misty pane, 'and surely to goodness I'd be more like to know than Will?'

'I'll do, thank ye. I'm right enough,' Sarah said stiffly, forced into speech at last; and Eliza laughed victoriously and returned to her food with zest.

'You've always been rarely strong, as far as I can think on. I never heard tell as you ailed anything in your life. You were always a rare hand wi' a knife and fork an' all!' she finished, laughing again. 'Will's a bonny fool to go scaring folk wi' such-like tales.'

'Yes, but we *did* go to the doctor's!' May broke out warmly, goaded into speech. 'Mrs. Thornthwaite's bothered with her eyes.'

Mrs. Will lifted her own sharply for a fresh stare at the defenceless face.

'Eh, now, you don't say so!' she exclaimed cheerfully, with a quite uninterested air. 'It's bad hearing, is that, but they look right enough, I'm sure.'

'They're bad, all the same!' May answered indignantly, on the verge of tears. 'Doctor says she ought to have an operation right off.'

There was a little pause after the dread word 'operation,' poignant in every class, but especially so in this. Even Mrs. Will was shocked momentarily into quiet. Her fork stayed arrested in mid-air, half-way to her mouth.

'Well, I never!' she observed at last, withdrawing her startled gaze. 'Eh, now, I never did!' She set to work again at her food like a machine that has been stopped for a second by an outside hand. 'I don't hold much by operations myself,' she went on presently, growing fluent again. 'I doubt they're never no use. They're luxuries for rich folk, anyway, seems to me, same as servants and motor-cars and the like. But you'll likely be asking somebody for a hospital ticket, so as you needn't pay?'

'Nay, I think not,' Sarah said calmly, though her hands gripped each other in her threadbare lap.

'You'll never go wasting your own brass on a job like yon!'

'Nay, nor that, neither.'

'You'll borrow it, likely?' A slyness came into her voice. She peered at Sarah over her cup.

'Nay.'

'Ay.'

'Ay, well, no matter where it come from, it would nobbut be money thrown away. You're an old body now, Sarah, and folk don't mend that much when they get to your age. It's real lucky you've only that small spot, as I said, and neither chick nor child to fret after you when you've gone.'

Sarah stood up suddenly when she said that, trying to focus her eyes on Eliza's face. She stood very stiff and straight, as if she were all of one piece from feet to crown. A sudden notion came to May that, if she had thrown off the shabby black cloak, a column of fierce flame would have shot up towards the roof. . . .

'I'll be saying good day, Eliza,' was all she said, however, and moved, but stopped because the other's skirts still lay before her feet. Mrs. Will leaned back in her chair, looking up at her, and smiled.

'Nay, now, Sarah, what's the sense o' getting mad? I'm real sorry about your eyes, but you'd ha' done better to tell me right off. As for saying good day and such-like so mighty grand, you know as well as me we're looking to see you at Blindbeck this afternoon.' She paused a moment, and then her voice rose on an insolent note. 'Ay, and you know well enough what you're coming for an' all!'

'Nay, then, I don't.' Sarah seemed actually to grow in height. She looked down at her quietly. 'Nay, I don't.'

'That's a lie, if I say it to all Witham!' Eliza cried in furious tones. Battle was really joined now, and her voice, strident and loud, carried into and disturbed even the street. Those near turned about openly to listen, or listened eagerly without turning. The man in the adjoining room got up and came to the door. May stood poised for flight, looking from one to the other of the warriors with dismay.

'You're leaving Sandholes, aren't you?' Eliza asked, exactly as if she were addressing somebody over the road—'leaving because you're broke! You're coming to Blindbeck to beg of Blindbeck, just as you've begged of us before. Simon told Will, if you want to know, and Will told me, and every farmer at market'll be taking it home by now. . . .'

There was a murmur of discomfort and

disapproval all over the room, and then somebody in a corner whispered something and
laughed. May roused herself and pushed her
way past Eliza with burning cheeks; but Sarah
stood perfectly still, looking down at the blurred
presence sneering from her chair.

'Ay, we're quitting right enough,' she answered
her in a passionless voice. 'We're finished, Simon
and me, and there's nowt for it but to give up.
But I've gitten one thing to be thankful for, when
everything's said and done . . . I'm that bad wi'
my eyes I can't rightly see your face. . . .'

The person who had laughed before laughed
again, and faint titters broke out on every side.
Sarah, however, did not seem to hear. She lifted
a thread-gloved hand and pointed at Eliza's
skirts. 'Happen you'll shift yon gown o' yours,
Eliza Thornthet?' she added, coolly. 'I've a deal
o' dirt on my shoes as I reckon you won't want.'

The laughter was unrestrained now, and Eliza
flushed angrily as she dragged her skirts reluctantly out of the way. From the corner of a
raging eye she observed the elaborate care with
which Sarah went by.

'We'll finish our bit of a crack at Blindbeck!'
she called after her with a coarse laugh; but
Sarah and May were already on the stairs. The
stranger put out his hand to them as they brushed
past, but in their anger and concentration they
did not notice that he was there. Even if he had
spoken to them they would not have heard him,
for through the cloud of hate which Eliza had
cast about them the voice of the Trump itself
would never have found a way. He stood aside,
therefore, and let them go, but presently, as if

unable to help himself, he followed them into the
street. They were soon cheerful again, he noticed,
walking at their heels, as the charm which they
had for each other reasserted its power. Once,
indeed, as they looked in at a window, they
even laughed, and he frowned sharply and felt
aggrieved. When they laughed again he turned
on his heel with an angry movement, and flung
away down the nearest street. He could not
know that it was only in their memories they ever
really laughed or smiled. . . .

VI

SIMON had been right in thinking that the tale of
the car would be all over the town by the time he
arrived. He came across it, indeed, almost the
moment that he got in. The driver of the car had
told a farmer or two in the inn-yard, and the
farmer or two had chuckled with glee and gone
out to spread it among the rest. Of course, they
took good care that it lost nothing in the telling,
and, moreover, the driver had given it a good
shove-off at the start. He told them that Simon
had shaken his fist and wept aloud, and that
Sarah had fainted away and couldn't be brought
round. A later account had it that the chase had
lasted fast and furious for miles, ending with an
accident in Witham streets. Simon encountered
the tale in many lengths and shapes, and it was
hard to say whether the flippant or sympathetic
folk annoyed him most. He always started out
by refusing to discuss the matter at all, and then
wouldn't stop talking about it once he had begun.
'Ay, well, ye see, I thought it was a hearse,'
he always growled, when forced to admit that

part of the tale, at least, was true. 'Mebbe I was
half asleep, or thinking o' summat else; or likely
I'm just daft, like other folk not so far.' Here he
usually threw a glance at the enquiring friend,
who gave a loud guffaw and shifted from foot to
foot. 'Ay, a hearse—yon's what I thought it was,
wi' nid-noddin' plumes, and happen a corp in
a coffin fleein' along inside. You've no call to
make such a stir about it as I can see,' he wound
up helplessly, with a threatening scowl. 'Boggles
isn't out o' date yet by a parlish long while, and
there's many a body still wick as can mind seeing
Jamie Lowther's headless coach and four!'

He forgot to feel annoyed, however, when he
found that his story had made him in some sort
the hero of the day. He could see folks talking
about him and pointing him out as he went along,
and men came up smiling and wanting a chat
who as a rule had no more for him than a casual
nod. Often, indeed, he had only a dreary time,
bemoaning his fate with one or two cronies almost
as luckless as himself; listening, perhaps, on the
edge of an interested group, or wandering into
some bar for a sup of ale and a pipe. But to-day
he was as busy as an old wife putting the story to
rights, and when he had stopped being angry for
having behaved like a fool, he began to feel rather
proud of himself for having done something
rather fine. He ended, indeed, by laughing as
heartily as the rest, and allowed several points
to pass which had nothing whatever to do with the
truth. He felt more important than he had done
for years, and forgot for a while the press of his
troubles and the fear about Sarah's eyes. Will
told himself that he hadn't seen him so cheerful

for long, and wondered whether things were really as bad at the farm as his brother had made out.

They made a curious couple as they went about, because in face and figure they were so alike, and yet the stamp of their different circumstances was so plain. They had the same thin face and dreamy eyes, lean figure and fine bones, but whereas one carried his age well and his head high, the other had long since bowed himself to the weight of the years. Will wore a light overcoat of a modern make, brown boots and a fashionable soft hat; but Simon's ancient suit was of some rough, hard stuff that had never paid any attention to his frame. Will had a white collar and neat tie; but Simon had a faded neckcloth with colourless spots, and he wore dubbined boots that had clogged soles, and a wideawake that had once been black but now was green. Eliza often observed in her kindly way that Simon looked old enough to be Will's father, but indeed it was in the periods to which they seemed to belong that the difference was most marked. Will had been pushed ahead by prosperity and a striving brood; while Simon had gone steadily down the hill where the years redouble the moment you start to run.

They had encountered the agent early on, and fixed an appointment for twelve o'clock; and afterwards they spent the morning together until noon struck from the Town Hall. Will had grown rather tired of hearing the hearse story by then, and felt slightly relieved when the time came for them to part. 'Nay, I'll not come in,' he demurred, as Simon urged him at the door of the 'Rising Sun.' 'You'll manage a deal better by yourself. You needn't fear, though, but what I'll see you through. We'll settle summat or other at Blindbeck this afternoon.'

But at the very moment he turned away he changed his mind again and turned back. 'I can't rightly make out about yon car,' he asked, almost as if against his will. 'What, in the name o' fortune, made you behave like yon?'

Simon muttered gloomily that he didn't know, and shuffled his feet uncomfortably on the step. Now that the shadow of the coming interview was upon him, he was not so perfectly sure as he had been that the story was a joke. He remembered his terror when the car was at his back, his frantic certainty that there were strange things in the air. He took it amiss, too, both as a personal insult and from superstition, that the Town Hall chimes should be playing 'There is no luck about the house' just as he stepped inside.

'It was nobbut a hired car, wasn't it,' Will went on—'wi' two chaps in it, they said, as come from Liverpool way?'

'That's what they've tellt me since,' Simon agreed, 'though I never see it plain. . . . Seems as if it might be a warning or summat,' he added, with a shamefaced air.

'Warning o' what?' Will threw at him with a startled glance. 'Nay, now! Whatever for?'

'Death, happen,' Simon said feebly—'nay, it's never that! I'm wrong in my head, I doubt,' he added, trying to laugh; 'but there's queerish things, all the same. There's some see coffins at the foot o' their beds, and you'll think on when last Squire's missis died sudden-like yon hard winter, she had it she could smell t'wreaths in t'house every day for a month afore.'

'Ay, well, you'd best put it out of your head as sharp as you can,' Will soothed him, moving away. 'You're bothering overmuch about the farm, that's what it is. A nip o' frost in the air'll likely set you right. Weather's enough to make anybody dowly, it's that soft.'

'Ay, it's soft,' Simon agreed, lifting his eyes to look at the sky, and wondering suddenly how long it had taken the gull to get itself out to sea. His brother nodded and went away, and he drifted unwillingly into the inn. The chimes had finished their ill-omened song, but the echo of it still seemed to linger on the air. They told him inside that Mr. Dent was engaged, so he went into the bar to wait, seating himself where he could see the stairs. The landlord tried to coax him to talk, but he was too melancholy to respond, and could only sit waiting for the door to open and summon him overhead. He was able to think, now that he was away from the crowd and the chaff about the hearse, but no amount of thinking could find him a way out. He had already given the agent a hint of his business, and would only have to confirm it when he got upstairs, but it seemed to him at the moment as if the final words would never be said. After a while, indeed, he began to think that he would sneak away quietly and let the appointment go. He would say no more about the notice to Mr. Dent, and things might take their way for another year. It was just possible, with the promised help from Will, that they might manage to scrape along for another year. . . .

He left it there at last and got to his feet, but even as he did so he remembered Sarah's eyes. He wondered what the doctor had said and wished he knew, because, of course, there would be no question of staying if the report were bad. He was still standing, hesitating, and wondering what he should do, when the door of the Steward's Room opened above, and a man came out.

It was, as somehow might have been expected, the stranger of the car, otherwise Simon's now celebrated 'hearse.' Simon, however, had not looked at him then, and he barely glanced at him now. It was a blind day, as Sarah had said, and all through the Thornthwaites seemed determined to be as blind as the day. The agent followed him out, looking cheerful and amused. 'I wish you luck all round!' Simon heard him say, as he shook the stranger's hand, and thought morosely that it was easy and cheap to wish folks luck. 'This should be the finest day of your life,' he added more gravely, looking over the rail, and the man going down looked up and said 'That's so!' in a fervent tone. The old farmer waiting in the bar felt a spasm of envy and bitterness at the quietly-triumphant words. 'The finest day of your life'—that was for the man going down. 'The heaviest day of your life'— that was for the man going up. With a touch of dreary humour he thought to himself that it was really *he* who was going down, if it came to that. . . .

With a feeling of something like shame he kept himself out of sight until the stranger had disappeared, and then experienced a slight shock when Dent called to him in the same cheery tone.

Almost without knowing it he had looked for the voice to change, and its geniality jarred on his dismal mood. Somehow it seemed to put him about at the start, and when Dent laid a hand on his shoulder, saying—'Well, Simon!' with a smile, it was all he could do not to give him a surly snarl by way of reply. They went into the old-fashioned room, which smelt of horsehair and wool mats, and Simon seated himself miserably on the extreme edge of a chair. Dent went to the window and lifted a finger to somebody in the street, and then seated himself at the table, and said 'Well, Simon!' and smiled again. He was a strongly built man, with a pleasant face, which seemed rather more pleasant than need be to his visitor's jaundiced eye.

He looked away from it, however, staring at the floor, and after the first conventional remarks began his tale of woe, that slow trickle of disaster which always gathered itself into terrible spate. 'You'll know what I'm here for, sir,' he concluded, at the end of his first breath, twisting his hat like a tea-tray in his restless hands. 'Things has got that bad wi' us I doubt we can't go on, and so we've made up our minds we'd best clear out next year.'

Dent nodded kindly in answer, but with a rather abstracted air. He had listened patiently enough to the slow tale, but Simon had a feeling that his tragic recital was not receiving the sympathy it deserved. He began a fresh relation of the ills which had befallen him at the farm, intending a grand climax to be capped by Sarah's eyes; but there were so many dead troubles to dig out of their graves as he went along, that the last and most vital dropped from the reckoning, after all.

'Ay, well, you've likely heard all this before,' he finished lamely in the middle of a speech, conscious that he had missed his point, though without being able to say how. 'We've had a bad year this year an' all, and I can't see as it's any use holding on. Me and my missis fixed it up as we come in, so, if you'll take my notice, sir, we'll go next spring.'

'Your wife's in town, is she?' Dent asked. For some reason he looked again at the window from which he had waved. 'How does she take the thought of leaving the farm?'

'Well, sir, we'll both feel it, after all these years, but I don't know as it's any use calling out. I put it to her as we'd best quit, and she agreed to it right off.'

'I wish you'd brought her along,' the agent said, still speaking in a detached tone. There were some notes on the table within reach of his hand, and he glanced thoughtfully at them as he spoke.

Simon stiffened a little, and looked surprised. 'I'm speaking for both on us, sir, as I said before.'

'Of course, Simon,' Dent said, rousing himself. 'I know that. But I'd have liked a word with her, all the same.' His glance went back to the notes, and he smiled as if at his own thoughts. . . . 'And so you've really made up your minds that you'd better go?'

'Haven't I been saying so, sir, all along?' Simon was really injured now, and his wounded dignity showed in his tone. Mr. Dent was taking the whole thing far too easily, he thought. First of all, he did not seem to be listening as much as he might, and then, when the notice was offered, he actually smiled! Tenants of forty years' standing do not look to have their departure speeded with smiles. Simon thought it heartless, to say the least, and only to be excused because Mr. Dent did not know what they had to face. They had not been very satisfactory tenants, of course —even Simon admitted that—and it was more than likely that the agent was rather relieved. At least he was saved the unpleasant task of turning them out, a duty which, as Simon knew, had seemed imminent more than once. But they were respectable folk of good stock, and they were not entirely to blame because they were failures, too. Gravity was their due, anyhow, if not sympathy, but Mr. Dent, on this solemn occasion, seemed to be failing them in both.

'Of course you know you're late with your notice?' he observed presently, looking up. 'You ought to have made up your minds a couple of months ago.'

'Ay, we're late, I know, but we weren't thinking of owt o' the sort then. I'm sorry if we've put you about, but you'll not have that much trouble in getting rid of the farm. It's nobbut a small spot, you'll think on. It'll let right off the reel.'

'It's been going back a long while, though,' Dent said thoughtfully, and then felt penitent as the old man flushed. Just for the moment he had forgotten that Simon was in the room.

'Of course I know you've had pretty rough luck,' he went on hastily, trying to cover it up. 'Sandholes holds the record for every sort of mischance. It sounds like one of the old fairy-tales,'

he added, laughing—'curses and all that! . . .
But I can't help thinking it would have been
better for everybody if there had been a change
earlier on.'

'Ay, well, you've gitten your change now, and
no mistake about it!' Simon retorted angrily,
deeply hurt. There was something wrong with
the scene, though he could not tell what it was.
He only knew that he had not expected it to go
in the very least like this.

'It should have been made long since if it was
to do you any good. . . .' Dent did not seem to
notice that there was anything amiss. He sat,
tapping the table, deep in thought, while Simon
seethed. . . . 'Sure you couldn't put on for another
year?'

This change of front upset his visitor so completely that he dropped his hat. He sat glaring
at Mr. Dent with a dropped mouth.

'Nay, then, I just couldn't!' he snapped at
last, wondering whether he was on his head or
his heels. 'Losh save us!' he added angrily,
'haven't I tellt you I meant to gang ever since I
come in? It'll take me all my time to hang on till
spring, as it is.'

'You've run it as close as that?' Dent enquired,
and Simon gave a grunt.

'Ay, and I'm not the first as has done it,
neither!'

'Couldn't your Blindbeck brother see to give
you a hand? He's done well for himself, I should
say, and his children are getting on.'

'He's given us a hand more than once already,
has Will, but there's no sense in throwing good
money after bad. We'll have to quit, next year,

if we don't this. Farm's going back, as you say, and I'm over old to pull it round. I can't keep going for ever, nay, nor my missis, neither.'

He remembered Sarah's eyes as he spoke, and how they were enough to clinch the matter in themselves, but he was too offended even to mention them by now. There was no telling to-day how Mr. Dent would take the tragic news. He had smiled and looked cheerful over the notice to quit, but Simon felt he would not be able to bear it if he smiled at Sarah's eyes. Indeed, it was all he could do to keep a hold on himself, as it was—first of all hearing that he ought to have gone long since, and then being told to stop when he'd settled to clear out!

The trend of his injured thought must have reached the other at last, for he roused himself to look at his sulky face.

'You needn't think I'm trying to shove the place down your throat!' he said, with a laugh. 'But I certainly thought you'd rather be stopping on!'

Simon felt a little appeased, though he took care not to show any sign. He growled miserably that they had never intended to quit except under a coffin-lid.

'This is where you want a lad of your own to take hold—a lad with a good wife who would be able to see to you both. You've no news, I suppose, of that son of yours that went overseas?'

'A word or two, now and then—nowt more. Nowt as'd set you running across t'countryside to hear.'

'No chance of getting him home again, is there?' Dent ventured, and Simon stared at the floor and shook his head. He must have felt a change in the atmosphere, however, for suddenly he began to repeat what Sarah had told May, how Geordie had written for money, and there had been none to send. The words came easily after he had made a start, and for the time being he forgot his resentment and injured tenant's pride.

'I reckon you know, sir, how it all come about. There'll ha' been plenty o' folk ready to tell you, I'll be bound, and them as knowed least'll likely ha' tellt you most. We never had but the one lad, Sarah and me, and, by gox! but he was a limb! The queer thing was that my brother Will's eldest should ha' been the very marrow o' mine—looks, voice, ways, ay, and character an' all. Will and me were whyet enough lads, I'm sure; it was terble strange we should breed a pair o' rattle-horns like yon. You couldn't rightly say there was any harm to 'em, but they were that wick they mun always be making a stir. Being that like, too, helped 'em rarely when there was chanst o' their getting catched. Each on 'em had a call for telling when he was about. Jim's was a heron like, but Geordie's was nobbut a gull. . . .'

This time it was his own glance that went to the window, as again he remembered the bird gone out to the waves. When Dent spoke, his mind came back from its flight with a tiny jerk.

'Then they made off to Canada, didn't they, the two lads? You told me something about it when I first came.'

'Ay, they cleared off in a night without a word or owt, and they've never done no good from then to this. Sarah sticks to it Geordie would

never ha' gone at all if it hadn't been for Jim, and
Will's missis sticks to it t'other way about. I
reckon there was nowt to choose between 'em
myself, but my missis never could abide poor Jim.
He was that set on her, though, there was no
keeping him off the spot. Right cruel she was to
him sometimes, but she couldn't drive him off.
He'd just make off laughing and whistling, and
turn up again next day. Of course, she was
bound to have her knife into him, for his mother's
sake. She and Eliza have always been fit to
scratch at each other all their lives.'

'Long enough to finish any feud, surely, and
a bit over? It's a pity they can't bury the hatchet
and make friends.'

'They'll happen make friends when the rabbit
makes friends wi' the ferret,' Simon said grimly,
'and the blackbird wi' the cat! I don't say Sarah
isn't to blame in some ways, but she's had a deal
to put up wi', all the same. There's summat
about Eliza as sets you fair bilin' inside your
bones! It's like as if she'd made up her mind to
pipe Sarah's eye straight from the very start. She
never said ay to Will, for one thing, till Sarah
and me had our wedding-day fixed, and then
danged if she didn't make up her mind to get
wed that day an' all! She fixed same church,
same parson, same day and same time—ay, an'
there's some folk say she'd ha' fixed on t'same
man if she'd gitten chanst!' He paused for a
moment to chuckle when he had said that, but
he was too bitter to let his vanity dwell on it for
long. 'She tellt parson it was a double wedding
or summat o' the sort, but she never let wit on't
to Sarah and me until she was fair inside door.

Sarah and me walked to kirk arm in arm, wi' nowt very much byordinar' on our backs; but Eliza come scampering up in a carriage and pair, donned up in a white gown and wi' a gert, waggling veil. Will was that shammed on it all he couldn't abide to look me in t'face, but there, I reckon he couldn't help hisself, poor lad! Sarah was that wild I could feel her fair dodderin' wi' rage as we stood alongside at chancel-step. She was that mad she could hardly shape to get her tongue round Weddin' Service or owt, and when we was in t'vestry I see her clump both her feet on the tail of Eliza's gown. She would have it nobody knew she was as much as getting wed at all—they were that busy gawping at Eliza and her veil. She was a fine, strapping lass, Eliza was, and I'd a deal o' work keeping my eyes off'n her myself! . . . ay, and I won't say but what she give me a sheep's eye or so at the back o' Will, as well. . . .' He chuckled again, and his face became suddenly youthful, with a roguish eye. 'But yon was no way o' starting in friendly, was it, Mr. Dent?

'Ay, well, things has gone on like that atween 'em more or less ever since, and I won't say but Sarah's gitten a bit of her own back when she's gitten chanst. Will having all the luck and such-like hasn't made things better, neither. Blind-beck's ganged up and Sandholes has ganged down—ay, and seems like to hit bottom afore it stops! Will and me have hung together all along, but the women have always been at each other's throats. It riled Eliza Jim being always at our spot, and thinking a deal more o' Sarah than he did of her. Neither on 'em could break him of it, whatever they said or did. He always stuck to it Sandholes was his home by rights.'

'Pity the two of them aren't here to help you now,' Dent said. 'Those runabout lads often make fine men.'

'Nay, I doubt they've not made much out, anyway round.' Simon shook his head. 'Likely they're best where they be,' he said, as Sarah had said on the road in. He sat silent a moment longer for politeness' sake, and then was stopped again as he rose to go.

'May I enquire what you intend to do when you leave the farm?'

The old man's face had brightened as he talked, but now the shadow came over it again.

'I can't rightly tell, sir, till I've had a word wi' Will, but anyway he'll not let us come to want. He's offered us a home at Blindbeck afore now, but I reckon his missis'd have summat to say to that. Ay, and mine an' all!' he added, with a fresh attempt at a laugh. 'There'd be lile or nowt done on t'farm, I reckon, if it ever come about. It'd take the lot on us all our time to keep them two apart!'

Again, as he finished, he remembered Sarah's eyes, and once again he let the opportunity pass. He was on his feet now, anxious to get away, and there seemed little use in prolonging this evil hour. Mr. Dent would think they were for ever whingeing and whining, and like enough calling out before they were hurt. . . . He moved hurriedly to the door, conscious of a sense of relief as well as of loss, and Sarah's eyes missed their final chance of getting into the talk. . . .

'You're likely throng, sir,' he finished, 'and

I'll not keep you.' He put a hand to the latch. 'Anyway, you'll kindly take it as we'll quit next year.'

Dent said—'No, Simon, I shan't do anything of the sort!' and laughed when the other shot round on him again with open mouth. His expression was grave, however, as he ended his speech. 'I want you to think it over a bit first.'

Simon felt his head going round for the second time. The red came into his thin face.

'I don't rightly know what you're driving at, sir,' he said, with a dignified air. 'I reckon I can give in my notice same as anybody else?'

'Oh, Lord, yes, Simon! Of course.' Dent's eyes went back to the notes. 'Yes, of course you can.'

'Ay, well, then?' Simon demanded stiffly. 'What's all this stir?'

'Well, . . . it's like this, you see . . . you've missed your time. It was due a couple of months back, as I said before.'

'Ay, but you're not that hard and fast about notice, as a rule! Tom Robison did t'same thing last year, you'll think on, and you let it pass. Seems to me you're by way of having a joke wi' me, sir,' he added, in a pitiful tone, 'and I don't know as it's kind, seeing how I'm placed.'

Dent jumped to his feet and came across to lay a hand on his arm.

'It's only that I've a feeling you'll change your mind, Simon,' he said earnestly, 'and you'll be sorry if you've spread it about that you're going to quit. A week, say—a week won't make that much difference, will it? Can't you let it stand over another week?'

'You said a minute back 'twas a pity we'd stopped so long! I can't make out what you're at, Mr. Dent—I'm danged if I can!'

The agent laughed and left him to stroll back again to the window, where he stood looking down into the full street.

'Perhaps we're neither of us as clear in our minds as we might be!' he observed, with a curious smile. 'The weather, perhaps; it's only a dreary day. I'm not one of the folks who like November grey.'

'Tides is big an' all,' Simon found himself saying, unable to resist the lure. 'We've had t'watter up agen t'wall every night this week. Last night I went out for a look afore it was dark, but it was that thick it was all I could do to tell it was there at all. There was just summat grey-like lifting under my nose; but, by gox! it was deep enough for all it was so whyet!'

Dent shivered at the drear little picture which the other had conjured up.

'I don't know how you sleep,' he said, 'perched on the edge of things like that! It would give me fits to have the sea knocking twice a day at my back door.'

'Ay, it knocks,' Simon said slowly, with a thoughtful air. 'There's whiles you'd fair think it was axing for somebody to come out. . . . You'll mind yon time you were near catched by the tide?' he went on, after a pause. 'Eh, man, but I was in a terble tew yon neet!'

'It was my own fault,' Dent returned—'not that it was any the nicer for that! I knew the time of the tide, but I'd forgotten the time of day. It was a day something like this, much the same dismal colour all through. Lord, no!' He shivered again. 'I've not forgotten, not I! I'll never forget pounding away from that horrible wave, and finding myself, quite without knowing it, back below the farm!'

'It was my missis saved you, yon neet,' Simon said, 'and a near shave it was an' all! Tide would ha' gitten you even then if it hadn't been for her. We heard you hollerin' and come out to look, but we couldn't see nowt, it was that dark. I thought we'd fancied it like, as we didn't hear no more, but Sarah wouldn't hear of owt o' the sort. She would have it she could see you liggin' at bottom o' t'bank, and she give me no peace till I'd crammelled down to look.'

'Well, you may be sure I'm grateful enough,' the agent said, as they shook hands. 'I wouldn't wish my worst enemy a death like that. I hope it's been put to the credit side of her account.'

He followed this caller out as he had done the last, and again, leaning over the railing, he called 'Good luck!' Simon, looking up, full of resentment, saw the face above him bright with smiles. He went out with offended dignity written in every line.

ELIZA

I

IT was two o'clock and after before the old folks left Witham. Simon had gone to his dinner on quitting the agent, and at his favourite eating-house he encountered others who wanted the hearse-story at first hand. He was not at all averse to talking about it by now, and after a good dinner it improved with the telling every time. Once more he forgot the interview of the morning as well as the coming one in the afternoon, and stayed smoking and talking and sunning himself in the fine atmosphere of success.

Sarah, however, had neither pipe nor admiring circle to soothe or enliven the heavy, dragging hours. She went into the inn after the 'Ship' dog-cart had rattled off, and tried to gather a little comfort from the parlour fire; but the glamour of the morning had departed with May, and now that she was alone she felt depressed and tired. The doctor's verdict, which had passed her by at the time, rushed back upon her, shaking her nerves and chilling her heart. She began to wonder what it would be like to be really blind, and in a sudden panic she made a strained attempt to discern the pictures and almanacks in the room, tracing the patterns of the anti-macassars with a shaking finger, and the shapes of the chair-backs and table-legs. When she was really blind, Simon would have to do for her instead of her doing for him, but he would only make a poorish job of it, she felt sure. There would still be plenty for both of them to do, in

spite of the fact that 'things had come to an end.'
There were the long winter months to be got
through before they left, as well as the work and
worry of changing house. May would help her,
no doubt; she could always count on May; but
she knew that she did not want to owe her more
than she could help. It was partly a new uprising
of dead jealousy, of course, as well as pride refusing dependence upon one who did not belong.
But at the back of all there was a more just and
generous motive than either of these—the consciousness that May had given too much already,
and should not be called upon for more.

Months ahead though it lay, she began presently
to think a woman's thoughts about the breaking-
up of the home. Little as they possessed of any
value in itself, there would be many things,
she knew, that they would want to keep. There
were certain things, expensive to renew, which
still had a flicker of useful life, and others, useless
to others as well as themselves, which were yet
bone of their bone and flesh of their ancient flesh.
She began to make a list in her head, and to
value the furniture as well as she knew how. She
had been to many a sale in her time, and had a
sufficiently good memory of what the things had
fetched, as well as of whose house had eventually
raked them in. She saw Sandholes full of peering
and poking folk, a chattering crowd stretching
into the garden and yard, and forming a black
procession along the roads of the marsh. She
saw traps and heavy carts and laden human
beings slowly departing with the stuff of her
human life; while the shreds that were left to her,
piled and roped on a waiting lorry, looked poorer

than ever in the light of day. She saw the garden gravel printed by many boots, and the yard trenched and crossed by wheels. She saw the windows open in a house from which nobody looked, and scrubbed, bare floors which seemed to have forsworn the touch of feet. She saw the lorry pass reluctantly away into the great, homeless place that was the world. And last of all she saw herself and Simon shutting the door that finally shut them out. There was all the difference in ten thousand worlds between the sound of a door that was shutting you in and the sound of the same door shutting you out. . . .

She had always been a still woman, when she had had time to be still, but she found it impossible to be still to-day. She began to walk up and down, listening for Simon's voice, and in the strange room she hurt herself against the furniture, and received little shocks from the cold surface of strange objects and the violent closing-up of the walls. She gave it up, after a while, forcing herself to a stand, and it was so that Simon discovered her when he opened the door at last.

She had a further wait, however, when he found that the trap had managed to oust the car from the coveted place. At first he was rather afraid that the hearse-story had earned him too many drinks, but even to marketing eyes the fact was plain. He chuckled as he walked from one to the other, saying 'Gox!' and 'Did ye ever now?' and 'Losh save us!' and 'Wha'd ha' thowt it!' The driver was not to be seen, or the wait might have been longer still, but as it was they were mounted presently on the emaciated seats, and

Simon jerked up the horse in a last spasm of victorious glee.

For some miles he talked of nothing but the sensation that he had caused in Witham, and how he had met with the hearse-story everywhere in the town.

'I'd nobbut to turn a corner,' he announced proudly, though pretending disgust, 'but sure an' certain there'd be somebody waiting to tax me on t'far side! There was Burton, and Wilson, and Danny Allen and a deal more, all on 'em ready wi'—"Well, Simon, and what about yon hearse?" I could see 'em oppenin' their mouths half a street off!' he chuckled loudly. 'Folk clipped me by t'arm and begged me tell 'em how it was, and t'others rushed out o' shops and fair fell on me as I ganged by!'

'They mun ha' been terble hard set for summat to do,' Sarah answered unkindly. 'What did you make out wi' Mr. Dent?'

At once the shadow fell again on the bright sun of Simon's success.

'Nay, you may well ax,' he growled, 'but I'm danged if I rightly know! He was that queer there was no doing owt wi' him at all. Seemed to be thinking o' summat else most o' the time— gaping out at winder and smiling at nowt. He was a deal queerer nor me, hearse or no hearse, and so I tell ye!'

'But you give notice in, didn't you! You likely got that fixed?'

'Well, I did and I didn't, after a manner o' speaking. I kept handing it in like, and he kept handing it back. He said we'd best take a bit more time to think.'

'We've had time and plenty, I'm sure!' Sarah sighed—'ay, that we have! . . . I reckon you tellt him about my eyes?'

Simon stirred uneasily when she mentioned her eyes, remembering how they had played in and out of his mind, but never once managed to come to the front.

'Nay, then, I didn't, if you want to know, because I never gitten chanst. I didn't rightly know what to say, neither, come to that. You catched doctor right enough, I suppose?'

'Ay, we hadn't to wait or owt. And he was right kind, he was that!'

'Happen he hadn't a deal to say, after all?' Simon enquired hopefully, and she gave a faint laugh.

'Nobbut that, if I didn't have an operation right off, I'd be as blind as a barn-door owl by next year!'

Simon said 'Gox!' and jerked the horse so violently that it nearly went through the hedge. 'Losh, missis, that's bad!' he went on dismally, when he had straightened out. 'It's worse than I looked for, by a deal. I've always been terble feared of operations and such-like. What's to be done about it, d'ye think?'

'Nowt.'

'Nay, but dang it!' he cried sharply—'we can't leave it like yon! If there's owt they can do for you, we mun let them try. They say some folk come out right enough, wi' a bit o' luck.'

'Luck isn't much in our way, I doubt,' she said, with a sigh, 'and it'd mean begging o' somebody, I reckon, and I've had enough o' that. May says there's free spots for such as us, but there's not

that much free in this world as I've ever seen.
I doubt it'd mean somebody's brass or other
going to pay for it in the end.'

'I could ax Will——' Simon began hurriedly,
without pausing to think, but she stopped him
before the well-known formula was out.

'Nay, then, master, you'll do nowt o' the sort,
so that's all there is about it! You're his brother,
and you've a right to do as you choose, but I'll
never take a penny piece from him if it's nobbut
for myself.'

'He'd have his hand in his pocket for you right
off. He's never been close about brass and such-
like, hasn't Will.'

'Ay, but it's Eliza's brass as well, you'll think
on, and *she's* close, right enough! She'd see me
blind and on t'streets afore she'd lift a hand, and
if happen she *did* lift it, I'd strike it down! Nay,
master, you can ax what you like for yourself,
but you'll ax nowt for me. As for the farm and
Mr. Dent, we're bound to get shot of it now,
whatever happens. The sooner things is fixed the
better I'll be suited, so I'll thank you to get 'em
seen to as soon as you can.'

''Tisn't my fault they're not fixed this very
minute!' Simon grumbled, feeling hardly used.
. . . 'Did you happen across Eliza in Witham?'
he asked her suddenly, after a while.

Sarah laughed faintly again, though this time
it was an echo of triumph.

'We'd a few words together in t'caif,' she
answered tranquilly, 'and wi' a few folks looking
on an' all. She was setting it round we were
broke, and had gitten the sack, and a deal more;
but I reckon I give her summat to bite on afore

I was through. . . . Seems as if you an' me had been having a sort o' side-show,' she finished, with a grim smile. 'Ay, well, we've given Witham summat to crack about, if we've never done nowt else. . . .'

Their minds had been full of Eliza as they drove to market, and now they were busy turning her over in their minds again. Sarah's account of her splendid effort cheered and uplifted them for a while, but they knew only too well that their sense of superiority would not last. Even their victories, ever so dearly bought, turned to Eliza's advantage in the end. Life was on the side of Eliza, for whom all things were certain to work out well. Heaven was on the side of Eliza, whose face had never registered a single memory of pain. The Simon Thornthwaites never got over the feeling that somehow she had played them false; had wheedled by undue influence the balance of justice off the straight. Alone, they were able to see some dignity in their tragic lives, but once with Eliza they were suddenly cheap— mere poor relations fawning at her skirts. They saw themselves framed as such in her mocking eyes, and felt for the moment the shameful thing they seemed.

She mocked them—that was the evil thing she did; that petty, insidious crime which human nature finds so difficult to forgive. Mockery by comparison was her method, and one which was almost impossible to fight. In all that Eliza said and did, by her attitude and her dress, she invited the world to mark the incredible gulf that yawned between the Simon Thornthwaites and the Wills. She had made her opening point on the double wedding-day, though the actual cause of the enmity lay farther back than that. Eliza, indeed, had intended to marry Simon and not Will— Simon, the elder, the better-looking, and even the smarter in those far-off days. But in this, at least, Sarah had won the fall, and Eliza had never recovered from her surprise. From that moment the spoilt beauty had seen in the other's plain person an opponent worthy of her steel, an antagonist whom it would take her all her life to down. Sneer and strike as she might, she could never be quite sure that she had finally got home, and in mingled inquisitiveness and wrath she sneered and struck again. There must be an end sometime to this spirit that would not break, but even after forty years there was little sign. Something deathless in Sarah rose up again after every stroke, and was always left standing erect when her world was in the dust.

Sarah thought of her wedding-day as they drove through the torpid afternoon, and under the low sky that was shut over the earth like a parsimonious hand. The wedding-day had been soft and sunny and sweet, with a high blue sky that looked empty from zone to zone, until, looking up until you were almost blind, you saw that you stared through layer upon layer of tender-coloured air. The mountains had been like that, too, clear yet vapour-veiled, and even the blue of the sea had been just breathed upon as well. It was a real bridal day, with its hint of beauty only just withheld, its lovely actual presences that still dropped curtains between. The earth-veils had had nothing in common with Eliza's flaunting mockery of a veil, nor was there anything in common between the mysteries behind. The strong mountain was more subtle and shy than Eliza, the terrible sea more tender, the great sky with its hidden storms more delicate and remote. Eliza's bold and confident beauty had clashed with them as a brass band clashes with a stretching, moonlit shore. It was for Sarah in her stiff straw bonnet and brown gown that the bridal veils of the world had been sweetly worn.

She had thought herself neat and suitable when she looked in the glass, and had found it enough, because all her instincts were neat and plain. It was a cruel irony of fate that had forced her into a morbid, passionate groove. In those days she had never as much as heard of obsessions of the mind, and would not have believed they could touch her, if she had. She had asked nothing of life but that it should be clean and straight, and still found it hard to believe in the shadowed, twisted thing which it had proved.

Her parents had died before Simon had made her a home, so she had gone out to service and had been married from her 'place.' She found him waiting when she went downstairs, in clothes as neat and suitable as her own, and he had given her a bunch of lilies of the valley, and a little Prayer Book with a brown back. They had always been matter-of-fact as lovers, and they were very matter-of-fact now, but Sarah, from this far-off distance, knew that, after all, they had not missed the thrill. Even in the small-windowed, silent house that had a maiden lady for tenant there was a touch of the exquisite thing —the same delicate rapture that was spreading its diaphanous wings over the coloured sea and land. . . .

They walked to church by the path across the fields, and the cattle raised their heads to look at Simon's suitable clothes, and the inch of escaped ribbon frisking on Sarah's suitable bonnet. They went arm-in-arm through the still churchyard, where their forefathers, lying together, saw nothing strange in this new conjunction of old names; and arm-in-arm up the empty aisle towards the cave of the chancel that had the flower of its rose window set in it like a jewelled eye. Their boots sounded terribly loud on the uncarpeted tiles, and they trod on tiptoe when they crossed the stones of the vaults, because the names looking up seemed somehow to turn into the uplifted faces of the prostrate dead. And presently the stone of the chancel-steps had stopped them as with a bar, bidding them think, in that last moment, whether the feet of their purpose had been rightly set.

They felt very small as they waited among the climbing pillars and under the spring of the groined roof; smaller and smaller as the unmarked minutes passed and nobody came. A shaft of light from the clerestory touched them like the point of a sacrificial knife, showing their faces humble and patient and a little too anxious to be glad. A bird flashed in through the open chancel-door, sat for a moment on the altar-rail and sang, and then caught sight of the sunlit country and flashed out again. It had not even seen the waiting couple who were so very quiet and so terribly small. And then, just as they were at their smallest the Pageant of Eliza had swept in.

There were many to tell them afterwards of the
sensation in the village when Eliza in gorgeous
apparel had come driving with trampling horses
to the old lych-gate. At the sound of the horses'
hoofs and the first flash of the veil the houses had
emptied themselves as a teapot empties itself when
you tilt the spout. Veils were the prerogative
of the 'quality' in those days, and that in itself
was sufficient to make a stir. In a moment there
were groups on the green, children running up
the street and folk pressing into the churchyard,
and in a moment more the veiled yet flaunting
figure had passed into the church, an over-rigged
ship up the straight estuary of the aisle.

Behind Simon and Sarah the place was suddenly full of noise, whispering and shuffling and
treading of heavy feet, and the ringing of nailed
boots on the smooth tiles. Presently all that had
been inside the church had gone out as if swept
by a broom, and all that had been outside had
come in with a blatant rush, filling it with curious
faces and crowded bodies and suppressed laughter
and muttered speech. Into the quiet hour that
had been meant for Simon and Sarah alone,
Eliza came full tilt with a tumult of sightseers in
her train. Not for her was the peace between the
springing pillars which rent before her like a curtain rent by hands. She trod with bold, self-
satisfied strides over the dead faces which to her
were only names. She created a vulgar raree-
show out of the simple blessing of a tranquil God.

Only outside, the sea and the mountains kept
their mystery till the knot was tied. The sacred
hour of Simon and Sarah was withdrawn silently
into higher courts.

All that was human in Sarah, however, remained at the mercy of the broken hour below. Now and then she caught a glimpse of Eliza's face through the veil, or a gleam of her shining gown as she twisted and turned. She thought to herself savagely that Eliza looked a fool, but that did not prevent her from feeling, by contrast, a fool, too. Even Will, shy and ashamed, but tricked out in unaccustomed gauds, helped to point the comparison between the pairs. She remembered how her cheeks had burned and her heart battered and her knees shook, while she strained her ears for the least sign of mirth from the crowded pews behind. The whole parody of her precious hour was bitter beyond words, but it was the mocking distinction in clothes that went farthest home. For the rest of her life Sarah was sharply conscious of all that Eliza wore, and hated it right to the sheep that had carried the wool on its innocent back, and the harmless cotton-plant that had grown for her unaware.

Eliza sailed down the aisle again amid giggles and loud asides, but Simon and Sarah crept quietly out of the church by the door through which the singing-bird had flown. They stood in the grass among the rose-bushes on the graves, and watched Eliza drive triumphantly away. The parson followed them out to make a kindly speech, which they were far too angry and humiliated to hear. He wanted to tell them that God had certainly liked them best, but he knew they would not believe him if he did. They were so certain that it was Eliza who had had the beautiful hour. They were too simple to know that it

was only they who had any of the beauty to carry
home. . . .

II

ALL their lives Simon and Sarah had been the vic-
tims of Eliza's Method. Nothing they had, horse,
cow, or cart, but was sooner or later measured
by Blindbeck standards and condemned. Their
furniture figured in Eliza's talk as often as her
own—their humble horsehair abased by her
proud plush, her stout mahogany lording it over
their painted deal. They had scarcely a cup or
plate, garment, beast, or crop, but it was flung in
the scale and instantly kicked the beam. People
grew tired of Eliza's Method after a while, but,
long before they had ceased to enjoy it, its work
was done. By that time they knew to the last inch
exactly how the Simon Thornthwaites had fallen
behind the Wills. The Simons were stamped in
their eyes as poor relations to the end of time,
and they treated them differently, spoke to them
casually, and as often as not forgot that they were
there. But Simon and Sarah did not forget, or
cease to notice, or cease to be hurt. Always they
felt pilloried by Eliza's blatant cry—'Look here,
upon this picture, and on this!'

Only in one respect had Sandholes and the
Simons ever managed to hold their own. Simon's
son had been every whit as fine as Will's, for all
the wooden spoon that was hanging over his
cradle. It was true that more and more children
came to Blindbeck, passing Sandholes by, but
that was nothing to Sarah as long as Geordie
was at hand. Geordie alone seemed more than
sufficient to right them in the eyes of an Eliza-
magicked world. He was a rattlehorn and a

limb, but he had stuff in him, all the same, and sooner or later he would prove that stuff to the world and the lordly Wills. All the working and scraping of those years went to the one passionate purpose of doing Eliza down. Those were the happiest years of Sarah's life, because for the time being she had a weapon against her foe.

Yet even here she found herself mocked by the amazing likeness between the brothers' sons. It had an uncanny effect upon her, as of something not quite human; even, indeed, as if there were something evil at its back. She had an uneasy feeling that, in some mysterious way, this was still another expression of Eliza's malice. The pride of stock in Simon and Will was stirred by this double evidence of breed; but Sarah, when people mistook the lads, was fretted to fierce tears. There were times when she even hated the smile on Geordie's lips, because of its exact similitude on Jim's. Most of all she hated herself when the wrong lad called, and she answered before she knew, or waved to a figure over the sands, and it came laughing and was not her son. . . .

She had much the same sense of something not quite canny about Jim's extraordinary passion for Sandholes and herself. It was almost, indeed, as if she feared it; as if she knew that in the future it might do her harm. Even she was not always proof against his laughing, kindly ways, and nothing but some such fear of a clutching love could have made her steel her heart. Through all her absorption in her splendid Geordie she could not help guessing at the greater depths in Jim. Geordie had yet to learn in exile what Jim had learned on the very threshold of his home. She remembered nursing him through an illness much against her will, and even now she could not shed that clinging memory and its appeal. . . .

It was perhaps because of this hidden terror that she never used his affection for her against his mother. She was often tempted to do so, for Eliza was sore in spite of her loud denials, and when the Method was hard at work on the furniture or the crops, it would have been pleasant to give her news—and generally none too pleasing news—of Jim. Often enough the words were on her tongue, but she never spoke them. Always something held her back from taking this easy means to strike.

Her ironic reward, however, was such as might well have made her think herself bewitched, for even out of her self-denial it was Eliza who gathered triumph. As time went on, and more and more lads appeared at Blindbeck, she deftly changed her tactics by a single twist of the wheel. She handed over to Sandholes, as it were, the one member of the Blindbeck family that did not come up to Blindbeck standards. Not that she ever said as much in words, or relinquished any claim that was likely to be of use. She merely contrived to convey the impression that he belonged by nature more to the Have-Nots than the Haves, to the penniless Simons rather than the wealthy Wills. The impression hardened, however, after the lads had run away, and Jim had finally nailed his sympathies to the mast. His father, indeed, did not give him up without a struggle, but Eliza became ever more detached from the wastrel who was her son. Smilingly, so to speak, she dropped

her thumbs and let him go. It was not long
before strangers were thinking him Simon's son
instead of Will's, and presently even Sarah awoke
to the fact that she was saddled with the Blindbeck failure as well as her own.

It was a smug young cousin of Eliza's who
finally opened her eyes, at one of those family
feasts which Simon and Sarah were always expected to attend. Eliza was never at her brightest
and best without them, as she very rightly said—
the organ-grinder without his necessary monkey,
the circus-master without his jumping clown.
As usual, the Simon Thornthwaites heard their
belongings catalogued and found utterly wanting, and, as usual, for the time being, shared the
general sentiment that they were beneath scorn.
The comparisons, passing in and out of shippon
and parlour, leaping from feather-bed to sofa,
and over root-crops and stacks of hay, arrived
finally at the missing sons.

'Our Harry's for learning the violin,' Eliza
informed the tea-party, swelling with conscious
pride. 'Master wouldn't hear tell o' such a thing
at first, but me and the girls talked him round
between us. I reckon he'll be suited all right,
though, when he hears our Harry play. Ah, now,
Sarah, but wouldn't that ha' been just the thing
for Geordie-an'-Jim? They were that fond o'
music, the poor lads, though they'd no more tune
to the pair on 'em than a steam-whistle. Eh,
well, poor things, fiddle-playing and such-like
wouldn't ha' been no use to 'em where they're at.
Brass wasted, that's what it would ha' been, so
it's just as well. . . .'

Harry, also swelling with pride, looked for

some sign of admiration from his aunt, but did not get it. Eliza soothed him with a meaning glance.

'The trouble is you've got to keep your hands terble nice for the violin. Our Harry's terble set on keeping his hands nice. . . . Geordie-an'-Jim would never ha' come to such-like quality ways, would they, Sarah? I never see such hands as the two on 'em used to show at meals! I mind you said they got sent home that often from school, at last the folks took to washing 'em on the spot! I used to be right sorry for you, Sarah, I was that, wi' their gert finger-marks all over the walls and the chair-backs. It's queer how different folk shape, I'm sure, even when they're as you might say near-bred. Our Harry frames rarely at folding table-cloths and the like, and no more dirt to 'em when he's finished than if he was a lass!'

The town-bred cousin gazed complacently at his hands, and observed that, if Geordie-an'-Jim were in Canada, as he understood, from all accounts it was much the best place for them. Eliza nodded lugubriously, the tail of her eye on Sarah's unstirred face.

'Ay, they're in Canada right enough, and like to be—aren't they, Sarah?—for a goodish while yet. They wrote home as they'd sworn to make their fortunes afore they crossed the pond again, but fortunes isn't as easy come by as some folk seem to think. Me and Will likely know as much about it as most, having managed middlin' well, but even for the best o' folk it isn't as simple as it sounds. There's always somebody at you one way or another, wanting to share what you've earned wi' your own hands. You've just got to keep lifting your feet right high off the ground, or you'll have folk hanging on to your shoe-wangs all the time. Ay, Geordie-an'-Jim'll find as fortunes don't come that slape off the reel! 'Tisn't as if it was our Harry and Tom here, ay, and Bill and Fred an' all, as'll find everything ready for 'em when they want to start on their own. They'll step into good farms as if it was stepping out o' bed, and they'll have Blindbeck behind them and its brass as well. They'll have a bit o' their own, come to that; I started 'em saving-books myself. Eh, yes, they'll do right well, but I doubt there's never farm nor Post Office book as'll come to Geordie-an'-Jim!'

Later in the day, the smug cousin, trying to be kind, had inquired of Sarah whether Geordie-an'-Jim were twins. She was too angry at first to answer him at all, and by the time she managed to get her breath, her mood had changed. They were alone at the time, and even Sarah could sometimes laugh at herself when Eliza was out of sight. The touch of humour freed her heart for an instant, and at once it rose up and stood by the lad whose mother had cast him off. Jim was suddenly before her, with his tricks of affection and his borrowed face, his constant cry that he had been born at Blindbeck only by mistake. 'I'm *your* lad, really, Aunt Sarah,' she heard him saying, as of old. 'I'm your lad *really*, same as Geordie is!' Jim was forty, by now, but it was a child's voice that she heard speaking and couldn't deny. The cousin repeated his question, and she smiled grimly.

'Twins? Ay . . . and as like as a couple o' peas.

As like as a couple o' gulls on the edge o' the tide. . . .'

It was the only time in her life that she ever stood openly by Eliza's hated son. But perhaps even that one occasion may count in the final sum of things. . . .

III

Now they had left the high-road and were making south-east through the winding lanes. Their shoulders were turned to the sea, though in that lost world of the mist only the native could tell where the bay was supposed to lie. It was one of the dead hours, too, when even the salt goes out of the marsh-air, and no pulse in it warns you subconsciously of the miracle coming. Between the high-mounted hedges it was still and close, and beyond them the land rose until its dank green surface stood soft against the sky. All the way Simon looked at the land with a critical eye, the eye of the lover which loves and asks at the same time. He looked at the ploughland and knew the rotation through which it had run and would have to run again; at rich grass-land which seemed never to have known the steel, and fields which, at rest for a hundred years, still spoke to some long-rusted share. He loved it, but he thought of it first and foremost as good material for the good workman engaged on the only job in the world. It was always the land that he coveted when he came to Blindbeck, never the house. Eliza had made of the house a temple to the god of blessed self-satisfaction, but even Eliza could not spoil the honest, workable land.

The farm kept showing itself to them as they drove, a quadrangle of long, well-kept buildings backed by trees. When the sun shone, the white faces of house and shippon looked silver through the peeping-holes of the hedge, but to-day they were wan and ghostly in the deadening mist. The turned beeches and chestnuts were merely rusty, instead of glowing, and seemed to droop as if with the weight of moisture on their boughs. The Scotch firs on a mound alone, stark, straight, aloof, had more than ever that air of wild freedom which they carry into the tamest country; and the pearly shadow misting their green alike in wet weather or in dry, was to-day the real mist, of which always they wear the other in remembrance.

The farm had its back well into the grassy hill, and the blind river which gave it its name wound its way down to it in a hidden channel and went away from it in a hidden dip in a field below. There was water laid on at Blindbeck, as Sarah knew, with a copper cylinder in a special linen-room, and a hot towel-rail and a porcelain bath. Simon's particular envy was the electric light, that marvel of marvels on a northern farm. He never got over the wonder of putting his hand to the switch, and seeing the light flash out on the second to his call. Once he had sneaked out of the house on a winter's night, and in the great shippon had turned the lights on full. Eliza, of course, had been nasty about it when she heard, but Will had understood him and had only laughed. Later, swinging a lantern in his own dark shippon, Simon had thought of those switches with envious longing. He did not know that they had taken the warm glamour out of the place, and slain at a blow the long tradition of its beauty. The lantern went with him like a descended star as he moved about, and out of the cattle's breath wove for itself gold-dusted haloes. There had been something precious about it all before, some sense of mystery and long-garnered peace, but to-night he could only remember Blindbeck and its modern toy. For the time being he ceased to feel the pull of the sweetest chain in the world, which runs straight back through all the ages to the Child in the Bethlehem Stall. . . .

There was a billiard-table at Blindbeck, too, with more switches to tempt Simon, and a well-laid tennis-lawn in the neat garden by the stream. On the far side of the farm was a great highway running north and south, as well as a main-line station over the drop of the hill. It seemed as if everything was made easy for those who lived at Blindbeck, from the washing of pots and the moving of stock to the amusement and education of the young.

Folk who came to Blindbeck for the first time believed that at last they had found the farm of all their dreams. They called it an earthly paradise, a model miniature village, a moral object-lesson, a true home. They came to it between well-cropped fields, marked by trim hedges and neat stone walls, and through uniformly painted gates secure in hinge and hasp into a tidy yard. They looked with pleasure at the shining knocker on the green house-door, and the fruit-tree lustily climbing the warm south wall. They looked with delight at the healthy, handsome family, the well-placed buildings and the show of pedigree stock. They looked at Will as he went shyly by, and said that his wife was undoubtedly the better horse. They looked at Eliza and said that she was the housewife of romance. When they went away they told others of this paradise which was Blindbeck, and the others came in their turn and looked and said the same. But to Simon and Sarah it was plain purgatory and nothing else, and with each gate that they loosed they unloosed a devil as well.

There was a party at Blindbeck, this afternoon, as long custom might have led them to expect. It was part of Eliza's Method to gather people together when the poor relations were due. There was always a noisy crowd, it seemed to the Simons, when they were tired, or when they had any particular business to transact. On the day after the lads had flown, there had been an unusually large crowd, with faces that looked like masks to the parents' tired eyes. . . . Will was fond of young folk, and made no objection to the stream of 'company' passing beneath his roof. His shy, quiet eyes watched the young tide of life surging ahead, with Eliza floundering like a porpoise in its midst. He was content only to watch, but he was not stranded, like the thirsty Simons; the waves still lapped about his feet. He could see youth and the pride of youth without the sense of desolation which embittered his brother and took his brother's wife by the throat. Simon was always surly when he came to Blindbeck, while Sarah was like a bomb in the hand which any unconscious soul might throw. Will did not know that for them every lad that they looked at should have been Geordie, and each lass a lass of their own with Geordie's face. He was sorry and

sympathetic, but he did not know those things.
It was Eliza who knew, and used the knowledge
for her private ends. You could always be sure
that Eliza knew where your hidden things were
kept.

To-day, tired as they were with the hours in
town, and already reacting from their great
decision, a jovial party seemed more than they
could stand. Signs of it reached them as they
came to the last gate, making Sarah draw in
her lips and Simon scowl. The sounds seemed
intensified by the stillness of the day, crossing and
jarring the mood of Nature as well as that of the
approaching guests. Faces were pressed to panes
as they rattled up, but nobody came out to give
Sarah a hand down, or to offer to help Simon
with the horse. They were too common a sight to
arouse any interest or even courtesy in that house.

She climbed down gropingly, and he led the
horse away, leaving her standing, waiting, in the
empty yard. She stood with her back turned to
the kitchen window, conscious, though she could
not see them, of the eyes that were raking her
shabby figure through the glass. The sounds of
merriment burst out afresh, and she winced a
little, though she did not move. They were
laughing at her, she felt sure, but there was
nothing new to that. They often laughed, she
knew, since she had ceased to be able to stop
them with a glance. She shivered, standing there,
and her bones ached with the damp, but she was
in no hurry to enter the warm, crowded room.
It was better to shiver in the coldest spaces of
earth than to be shut into heaven itself with Eliza
and her tongue.

The green house-door with its brass knocker
was close at her left hand, but she did not attempt
to open it and go in. That was a privilege only
accorded to the rich and proud, not to a poor
relation come to beg. Nevertheless, it was one of
her hidden dreams that some day she would enter
by that grand front-door. In the Great Dream
Geordie came home with a fortune in his hands,
so that all doors, even the door of Blindbeck,
instantly stood wide. They would drive up to it
in a smart cart behind a fast young horse, with
Geordie, a pattern of fashion, holding the reins.
His mother would be beside him, of course, in
crackling silk, with a velvet mantle and a bonnet
of plumes and jet. Simon, the lesser glory, would
have to sit behind, but even Simon would be a
sight for Blindbeck eyes. When the dream came
true, the house could be as full of pryers as it
chose, with crushed noses and faces green with
envy set like bottle-ends in every pane. The
farm-men would come to the doors and gape,
and even the dogs would stop to sniff at so much
that was new. Geordie would jump down, reins
in hand, and bang the brass knocker until it
shook the house; while Sarah, secure in the
presence of her golden lad, would sit aloft and
aloof like any other silken queen. Soon they
would hear Eliza's step along the sacred, oil-
clothed passage; and she, when she opened the
door, would see their glory framed beyond. Sarah
would throw her a graceful word, asking leave
to step inside, and climb down with a rustle of
silk on the arms of her husband and son. She
would set her feet on the snowy steps, and never
as much as trouble to look for a mat. With a

smile she would offer her hostess a kindly, kid-gloved hand. In the whole armour of the successful mother she would bear down upon her foe. . . .

It was one of those things that seem as if they might happen so easily, and never do—never do. Simon returned presently, accompanied by Will, and they entered the house as usual through the old stone porch. No dog even looked aside at them as they crossed to the kitchen door. No portent of coming wonder shed a sudden sunlight on the day. The old trap was tipped on its shafts behind a sheltering wall. The old horse, himself mere waiting food for the nearest hounds, munched his way happily through his feed of Blindbeck corn.

Will talked shyly as he led the way, trying to brighten the melancholy pair.

'You must have a sup o' tea before we get to business,' he said to his brother, 'and Sarah can rest herself while we have our crack. We're over soon wi' tea to-day, but I reckon you won't mind that. You'll be tired, likely, and it's none so warm. I'll be bound Simon'll have a thirst on him, anyway!' he smiled to Sarah. 'He's done a deal o' tattling, Simon has, to-day!'

He could not get any response from them, however; indeed, they scarcely seemed to hear. The fear of Eliza was upon them, that was always so strong until they were actually in her presence; the same fear that had sent them scuttling like scared rabbits out of the Witham inn. Sarah was struggling with the usual jealous ache as they entered the spacious, cleanly place, with the kindly smell of new-baked bread filling the whole house. She knew as well as the mistress where

the kitchen things were kept, the special glories
such as the bread-maker, the fruit-bottler, and
the aluminium pans. The Blindbeck motto had
always been that nothing beats the best. Half
her own tools at home were either broken or
gone, and there was only a blind woman to make
shift with the rest as well as she could. Little
need, indeed, for a great array, with the little
they had to cook; and little heart in either cook-
ing or eating since Geordie had gone away. . . .

Will opened the door of the main kitchen, and
at once the warmth and jollity sweeping out of it
smote the shrinking visitors like an actual blast.
The party were already at table, as he had said,
and met the late-comers with a single, focussed
stare. It was one of their chief bitternesses, indeed,
that they always seemed to arrive late. Eliza was
at the back of it, they felt almost sure, but they
had never been able to discover how. No matter
how they hurried the old horse, asked the hour
of passers-by, or had Simon's old watch put as
right as it would allow, they never seemed to
arrive at the right time. They could not be
certain, of course, that she had watched for them
from upstairs, and at the first sign of their coming
had hustled the party into tea, but somehow
or other they knew it in their bones. Things
happened like that, they would have told you,
when you were up against Mrs. Will; things that
never by any chance would have happened with
anybody else.

The room was cloudy to Sarah as she went in,
but jealousy had long ago printed its details on
her mind. She knew what the vivid wall-paper
was like, the modern furniture and the slow-

combustion grate. Once it had been a beautiful
old house-place with a great fire-spot and a crane,
an ingle-nook, a bacon-loft, and a chimney down
which both sun and moon could slant a way.
Eliza, however, had soon seen to it that these
absurdities were changed, and Sarah, though she
affected contempt, approved of the changes in
her heart. It was true that she always returned
to Sandholes with a great relief, but she did not
know that its bare austerity soothed her finer
taste. She only knew that her mind expanded
and her nerves eased; and, though grief went
with her over every flag and board, a cool hand
reached to her forehead as she went in.

Simon included in one surly glance the faces
round the loaded table, the bright flowers, the
china with the gilded rim, and the new window-
curtains which he would never even have seen in
any house but this. 'Plush, by the look on 'em,
and the price of a five pun note!' he thought
resentfully, as he stood waiting to be given a
place, and wondering which of the people present
he disliked the most. There were the two Swainson lasses from the nearest farm, with their young
duke of a brother, who was in a Witham bank.
There was a Lancashire youth whom Will had
taken as pupil, and Stephen Addison and his
missis, who were both of them preaching-mad.
He held forth at chapel and she at Institute
meetings and the like, and folk said they kept
each other awake at nights, practising which of
them could do it best. There was Sam Battersby
of Kitty Fold, who never knew where his own
heaf ended and other people's began, and the
familiar smug cousin, long since formally pledged

to Eliza's eldest lass. There was a grandchild or
two, and of course the Blindbeck brood, with the
exception of a couple of married daughters and
the obliterated Jim. . . . It was small wonder,
indeed, that, after all those years, nobody missed
him in that upcoming crowd.

Eliza's hearty voice, that was never hearty at
core, rose like a strong-winged, evil bird at the
unwanted guests. The sight of them seemed to
surprise her so much that she dropped a gold-
rimmed cup.

'Surely to goodness, Simon and Sarah, yon's
never you! I'd give you up an hour back or
more, I had indeed. You've been a terble while
on t'road, surely—a terble while after us? But
there—I always forget how fast yon grand little
mare of ours gets over t'ground! You'd need
to start sooner than most folk wi' your poor old
crock.'

She broke off to throw a remonstrance at Will,
who was bundling two of his daughters out of
their seats to make room for their uncle and aunt.

'Nay, now, Will,' she called vexedly down the
table. 'What d'ye think you're at? Leave t'lasses
alone, can't you? Let the poor things be! If it's
a chair you're wanting, there's one here by me
as'll suit Sarah just grand. Sarah can't abide a
chair wi' a cane bottom—says it rubs her gown.
It's right enough, too, I'm sure, wi' velvet and
the like—(I made a bonny mess o' yon grand
gown I had when Annie Belle was wed)—but I
can't see as it'll do any harm to a bit o' poorish
serge. Anyway, Sarah can have the best plush
to set on, if she sets here, and, as for Simon, you're
for ever sticking him where I can't so much as

see the end of his nose! You're never thinking
I'm still sweet on him, surely,' she added, laughing, 'or that happen he'll be making sheep's eyes
at me, as he used to do?'

She looked at the young folk, and chuckled
and winked, and they nudged each other and
laughed, too. But Sarah did not laugh as she
waited behind the chairs, or Simon, red to the
ears, and recalling the machinations of Eliza's
youth. He pushed one of his nieces roughly out
of his way and took her place, while Sarah went
slowly to seat herself on the red plush chair that
was warranted not to hurt her poor patched
gown.

'I hope there's summat for you, I'm sure!'
Eliza went on, when the giggling and whispering
had died down, and Simon's thin cheeks had
lost their furious red. She cast an anxious glance
down the well-filled table, but her tone was com-
placency itself. 'Folks as come late can't expect
to find everything just so. . . . Ay, I give you up
a long while back. Sally here'll tell you I give
you up. "Sally," I says to her, "likely yon old
horse'll be put to it to do the extra bit, and so
they've happen thought better on't, and gone
straight home. You're that used to good horses,
Sally," I says, "you don't rightly know how poor
folks has to shift. Not but what they'll get a deal
better tea here than they will at home, Sally,"
I says, "and though I says it as shouldn't, that's
the truth! Ay, they'll come to tea, I'll be bound,
Sally," I says, but I changed my mind when I
thought on the old horse.'

Sarah said nothing in reply to this, partly
because her brain was swimming with the heat

of the room, but chiefly because she never did
say anything until Eliza was well ahead in the
race for speech. This course of action helped
her to reserve her strength, but at the same time
deepened the bitterness in her heart. It would
have been better for both of them if they could
have got the inevitable tussle over at the start;
exhaustion on both sides might have brought at
least a pretence at amity in its train. But it had
always been Sarah's instinct to hold herself back,
and time had turned the instinct into a fixed
need. For the moment, at least, her strength
was certainly to sit still.

'I doubt there's no tea for you just this minute,
Sarah,' Eliza said, affecting great concern as she
lifted the teapot lid. 'Sally, my lass, you'd best
see about mashing another pot. There'll be a
deal o' folk sending up for more in a brace o'
shakes, and we can't have them saying they're
not as well-tret at Blindbeck as they're used. Not
as anybody's ever said it yet as I've heard tell,
though you never know what folks'll do for spite.
Most on 'em get through their three cups afore
they're done, and me like as not just barely
through my first. Eh, but I used to be terble
bothered, just at the start, keeping folks filled
and their mugs as they rightly should! You barns
wasn't up then, of course, but we'd farm-lads in
the house, and wi' a rare twist to 'em an' all!
Yon's a thing you've never been bothered with,
Sarah, wi' such a small spot and lile or nowt in
the way o' work. You'd nobbut a couple o'
hands at any time, had you, and not them when
you'd Geordie-an'-Jim? You've a deal to be
thankful for, I'm sure, you have that! You've

always been able to set down comfortable to
your meat, instead o' fretting yourself to skin and
bone seeing as other folk had their wants.'

Here Mrs. Addison offered to pass her cup,
and then thought better of it, remembering the
new brew. Eliza, however, urged it forward.
Apparently she had discovered concealed virtue
under the teapot lid.

'Nay, now, Mrs. Addison, there's a sup in the
pot yet! You've no call to look shy about it—
I wasn't talking at you! . . . Pass Mrs. Addison
the cream, Mary Phyllis, and waken up and look
sharp about it! Blindbeck tea's none the worse,
I reckon, for a drop o' Blindbeck cream. . . .'
She returned the cup, smiling benignly, and then
pretended to have lost Sarah and suddenly found
her again. 'Losh, Mrs. Simon, you're that whyet,
I'd clean forgot you were there! You'll not want
to be waiting on Sally and the fresh brew. I'll
wet leaves again for you just to be going on with!'

So Sarah got the bottom of the pot, after a little
more talk, a hunt for a clean cup and an address
on the value of the spoons. Half a cup—consist-
ing chiefly of tea-leaves—was passed to Simon,
but was intercepted on its way by Will. Simon
did not notice the manœuvre, being busy glower-
ing at a niece's shoulder turned sulkily on him
from the left; but Eliza saw it from her end of the
table and turned an angry red. She never forgot
Simon's indifference to her as a girl, and would
have made him pay for the insult if she could. She
could not always reach him, however, because
of the family tie which nothing seemed able to
break. But Sarah, at least, it was always con-
soling to think, could be made to pay. There

were times when all her reserve could not hide
from a gleeful Eliza that she paid. . . .

So Simon got the new brew without even
knowing that it was new, while Sarah drank the
unpleasant concoction that was weak at the top
and bitter as sea-water at the bottom. Sally came
in with another great brown pot, and sat down
languidly at her aunt's side. She and the smug
cousin had been engaged for years, but there
seemed little prospect of the wedding taking
place. She had been a handsome girl, and was
good to look at still, but there were handsomer
Thornthwaites growing and grown up, as apparently the cousin was quick enough to perceive.
To-day he had found a seat for himself beside
Mary Phyllis, who kept glancing across at her
sister with defiant pride. Sally had a cheap town-
look, nowadays, the cousin thought, not knowing
that she had assumed it long ago to please himself. Now that he was more mature, he preferred
the purer country type of Mary Phyllis, as well
as the fresher atmosphere of her youth. Sally
talked to young Swainson, and pretended not
to care, but she was too unhappy to bother
about her aunt. The Simon Thornthwaites were
boring, at any time, like most permanently
unlucky people, and to-day she was too worried
even to try to be kind. So Sarah, after whom she
was called, and who was her godmother to boot,
got very little to eat and only the dregs of things
to drink; and nobody at all rose up to deliver
her from Eliza.

Mrs. Addison had opened her mouth very
impressively more than once, but it was only now
that she got a chance to speak. In spite of their

boasted fluency, both she and her husband had always to yield the palm to Mrs. Will. Mrs. Addison, however, always watched her chance, while Stephen was simply flabby, and did not try. She and Eliza in the same room were like firmly-opposing currents, flowing strongly in the same stream.

'Mr. Addison's to preach at this mission they're having, next week,' she announced proudly. 'There's to be a service for men only, and our Stephen's to give 'em a talk. I won't say but what he'll do as well as a real minister, even though I do happen to be his wife. Likely you'll think on about it, and send some of your lads along, Mrs. Will?'

Eliza was quite unable to conceal her disgust at a distinction achieved by somebody not her own.

'I'll do my best, I'm sure,' she assented casually and without looking at her, 'though I doubt they'll want coaxing a bit wi' a broom-handle or a clout!' She disliked being called Mrs. Will, and knew that Mrs. Addison did it with fell intent. It was galling to be reminded that, in spite of his success, Will had still not managed to make himself into the elder son. . . . 'I can't say they're that set on either church or chapel unless it's to see a lass,' she went on, busy with the cups, 'and I doubt they don't reckon much o' sermons unless they're good. They've been better eddi-cated than most folk, you'll think on, so they're hard to suit. 'Tisn't likely they could do wi' second-hand preaching from some as happen never went to school at all.'

Mrs. Addison made a sudden attempt to speak,

but choked instead, while Eliza looked as innocent as a large-sized lamb.

'Ay, I've heard a deal o' sermons as was just waste breath,' she went on kindly, 'and that's the truth. All the same, I'll likely look in at mission myself, one o' these days, if I can get away. I'm always glad to set still after a hard week, and to get a look at other folks' jackets and hats. Not that there's much to crack on at chapel, that way. . . . I'm a deal fonder o' church. I was wed at St. Michael's, you'll think on—ay, and Sarah an' all. Eh, I could laugh even yet at yon march we stole on her, me an' Will!'

Sally moved impatiently at her aunt's elbow, and muttered something under her breath. She was tired of the old story, and disapproved of it as well. Sarah had lifted her cup to her lips, but now she set it down. . . .

Mary Phyllis stopped giggling a moment, and leaned forward to speak.

'I was telling Cousin Elliman about it only this morning,' she said noisily, 'and he says it's the funniest thing he ever heard! I thought everybody knew about it, but he says he didn't. He said it was real smart of you, mother, and he wished he could have been there. . . .'

'I'll be bound Sarah didn't think it smart!' Eliza chuckled, but without glancing at her victim's face. She had a trick of discussing people when they were present, as Sarah knew. She could tell by the trend of Eliza's voice that she spoke without turning her head.

'Smart? Nay! Sarah was real wild, you take my word! I spoke to her in t'vestry when the show was through, and she give me a look as was

more like a dog's bite. Eh, well, I reckon poor
Sarah was jealous o' my gown, seeing her own
was nowt to crack on—and nowt then! I'd
always settled to be real smart when I got wed,
and my own lasses was just the same. None o'
my folk can do wi' owt as isn't first-class and
happen a bit over. Yon's the photo we had took
at Annie Belle's wedding,' she added, turning to
point, 'and there's another of Alice Evelyn's in
the parlour.'

The cousin and Mary Phyllis left their seats to
giggle together over the stiff figures, and presently
the girl turned to her sister with a malicious
taunt.

'I say, our Sally, you'd best look out when you
do get wed, or happen I'll play a trick on you,
same as mother did Aunt Sarah! You'll be rarely
riled if I come marching up the aisle with a fine
young man, taking all the shine out of you and
Elliman!'

The cousin said something in a low tone which
made her flush and laugh, and Sally guessed at it
quickly enough, though it did not reach her ears.
The tears came into her eyes, and on an impulse
of fellow-feeling she turned towards her aunt.
She was asking after May Fleming when her
mother broke across her talk.

'Eh, now, Sarah, yon was never May, was it,
along wi' you in Witham? I'll be bound I'd
never have known her if she hadn't been with
you, but there's not that many you're seen about
with nowadays at market. 'Tisn't like me, as
can't stir a step without somebody wanting a
crack or hanging on to my gown. But May's
changed out of all knowledge—I was fair bothered

to see her look so old! I'll swear our Annie Belle looks as young again, for all she's been wed a dozen year at least. Ay, I thought May terble old, and terble unmannerly as well. I'd be shammed to think as any lass o' mine had such-like ways. You weren't over-pleasant spoken yourself, Sarah, if it comes to that. The folk in the caif were laughing a deal after you'd gone out, and saying you must be wrong in the garrets to act so queer.'

Sarah had regained her spirit a little, in spite of her poor tea. She straightened herself on the plush chair and answered calmly.

'They can say what suits 'em and welcome, as long as they let me be. You know what put me about, Eliza, and nobody to thank for it but yourself. As for folks laughing and making game o' me and such-like, it was you they was sniggering at plain enough when I come out.'

Eliza's colour rose, but she struggled to keep her virtuous air. She looked at Sarah with a sorrowful eye.

'I wouldn't get telling lies about it, Sarah,' she observed kindly, 'I wouldn't indeed! Mrs. Addison's listening, think on, and she'll be rarely shocked at such-like ways. Caif-folk were shocked more than a deal, an' me just having a friendly talk an' all!'

'It's a queer sort o' friendliness as puts folk to open shame!' Sarah's colour was flying a flag, too. 'It's nobbut a queer sort o' friend as goes shouting your private business at the end of a bell!'

'There isn't a deal that's private, surely, about the mess o' things you've made on the marsh? . . .' The fight was really begun now, and Eliza turned

in her seat, fixing her adversary with merciless
eyes. Sarah could see very little but a monstrous
blur, but she felt her malignant atmosphere in
every nerve. She could hear the big, solid presence
creaking with malice as it breathed, and had an
impression of strained whalebone and stretching
cloth. But it was always Eliza's most cherished
garments that she visioned when they fought—
the velvet gown that was folded away upstairs . . .
gloves, furs, and a feathered hat; farthest of all,
the wedding-gown and the flaunting veil. . . .

'Private!' Eliza repeated the sneered word as
if it were something too precious to let go. 'There
can't be that much private about things as we've
all on us known for years. What, folks has puzzled
no end why you've never ended in t'bankruptcy
court long since! Will and me could likely ha'
tellt them about it, though, couldn't we, Sarah?
Will an' me could easy ha' tellt 'em why! Will
and me could ha' tellt where brass come from as
was keeping you on t'rails——'

Will had been lending a careful ear to Simon's
surly talk, but he lifted his head at the sound of
his name.

'Now, missis, just you let Mrs. Simon be!' he
admonished, with a troubled frown. 'You're
over-fond of other folks' business by a deal.'

'I'll let her be and welcome, if she'll keep a
civil tongue in her head!' Eliza cried. She went
redder than ever, and slapped a teaspoon angrily
on the cloth. 'But if our brass isn't our business,
I'd like to know what is, and as for this stir about
quitting Sandholes, it's nothing fresh, I'm sure!
We all on us know it's a marvel landlord didn't
get shot on 'em, long ago.'

The last remark galvanised Battersby into lively speech. Hitherto he had been busily concentrated on his food, but now his mean little features sharpened and his mean little eyes shone. He bent eagerly forward, leaning on the cloth, knife and fork erect like stakes in a snatched plot.

'What's yon about quitting Sandholes?' he asked, in a thin voice. 'Are you thinking o' leaving, Simon? Is it true?'

'I don't see as it's any affair o' yours, if it is,' Simon answered him, with a sulky stare.

'Nay, it was nobbut a friendly question between man and man. If you're quitting the farm, it would only be neighbourly just to give me a hint. There's a lad o' mine talking o' getting wed, and I thought as how Sandholes'd likely be going cheap. Has anybody put in for it yet wi' t'agent, do ye think?'

'Nay, nor like to do, yet awhile,' Simon answered glumly, full of sullen hurt. All his love for his tiresome dwelling-place rose to the surface at this greed. 'I don't mind telling you, Mr. Battersby, as you ax so kind, that I give in my notice but it wasn't took. Mr. Dent would have it I mun think it over a bit more. Your lad'll just have to bide or look out for somebody else's shoes.'

This dreadful exhibition of meanness aggrieved Battersby almost to the verge of tears.

'Well, now, if yon isn't dog-in-the-manger and nowt else!' he appealed to the company at large. 'What, you're late wi' your notice already, and yet you're for sitting tight to the farm like a hen on a pot egg! I shouldn't ha' thought it of you, Simon, I shouldn't, indeed. Here's a farmer wanting to quit and my lad wanting a farm, and

yet the moment I ax a decent question I get
sneck-posset geyly sharp. You're jealous, that's
what it is, Simon; you're acting jealous-mean.
You've nobbut made a terble poor job o' things
yourself, and you want to keep others from
getting on an' all!'

Simon gave vent to an ironic laugh.

'Nay, now, Sam, never fret yourself!' he jeered.
'You and your lad'll get on right enough, I'll be
bound, what wi' your heaf-snatching and your
sheep-grabbing and the rest o' your bonny ways!
What, man, one o' your breed'd be fair lost on a
marsh farm, wi' nowt to lay hands on barrin'
other folks' turmuts, and never a lile chance of
an overlap!'

Battersby's reputation was well known, and an
irrepressible laugh greeted Simon's speech, but
was instantly cut short by the terrible spectacle
of the victim's face. Only the smug cousin went
on laughing, because he was ignorant as well as
smug, and did not know what a heaf meant, let
alone how it was possible to add to it by Sam's
skilful if unlawful tricks. Battersby jumped to
his feet and thumped the table, so that the blue
and gold china danced like dervishes from end
to end. Mrs. Addison's tea made a waterfall
down her second-best bodice, and Sarah's heart,
not being prepared for the thump, leaped violently
into her mouth.

'I'll not be insulted in your spot nor nobody
else's,' he stormed at Will; 'nay, and I'll not take
telling from yon wastrel you call brother, neither!
All on us know what a bonny mess o' things he's
made at Sandholes. All on us know it'll be right
fain to see his back. . . . As for you, you gomeless

half-thick,' he added, swinging round so suddenly
on the smug cousin that he was left gaping, 'you
can just shut yon calf's head o' yours, and mighty
sharp, or I'll shut it for you! Them as knows
nowt'd do best to say nowt, and look as lile like
gawping jackasses as Nature'll let 'em!' . . . He
sent a final glare round the stifled table, and let
Eliza have the sting in his tail. 'I'd been looking
to be real friendly wi' Blindbeck,' he finished
nastily, 'and my lad an' all, but I don't know as
we'll either on us be fain for it, after this. Nay, I
wain't set down agen, missis, and that's flat, so
you needn't ax me! I'm off home and glad to be
going, and no thanks to none o' you for nowt!'

He glanced at his plate to make certain there
was nothing left, snatched at his cup and hastily
swallowed the dregs; then, thrusting his chair
backward so violently that it fell to the floor, he
clapped his hat on his head and marched rudely
out. Eliza, catching a glance from a tearful
daughter, got to her feet, too. They swam from
the room in a torrent of loud apologies and bitter,
snarled replies.

Will leaned back in his chair with a fretted
expression on his gentle face. The cousin, slowly
turning from red to mottled mauve, observed to
Mary Phyllis that the old man's language was
'really remarkably like my chief's!' Some of the
younger end started to giggle afresh, but Sarah
was still trembling from the unexpected shock,
and Simon felt gloomy again after his public
effort. He could see that he had upset Will, and
that was the last thing he wanted to do, to-day.
Will did not like Battersby, but he liked peace,
and there were other reasons for friendly relations

at present. Will's youngest daughter had a direct
interest in Battersby's lad and his hopes of a
farm, and now the father had shaken the Blindbeck dust from his proud feet. She looked across
at the cause of the trouble with tear-filled, indignant eyes.

'Seems to me things is always wrong when you
come to Blindbeck, Uncle Simon!' she exclaimed
hotly. 'Nobody wants your old farm, I'm sure!
I wouldn't have it at a gift! But you might have
spoken him fair about it, all the same. I never
see such folks as you and Aunt Sarah for setting
other folk by the ears!'

Will said 'Whisht, lass, whisht!' in as cross a
tone as he ever used to his girls, and Simon
glowered at her sulkily, but he did not speak.
She was a fair, pretty thing, with Geordie-an'-
Jim's eyes, and he did not wish to injure her
happiness in any way. It was true enough, as
she said, that there was generally something in
the shape of a row as soon as he and Sarah set
foot in the house, but he could not tell for the
life of him how it came about. It could not be
altogether their fault, he thought resentfully, yet
with a sort of despair. To-day, for instance, he
had every reason for keeping the peace, and yet
that fool of a Battersby must come jumping down
his throat! Nobody could be expected to stand
such manners and such nasty greed—grabbing a
man's homestead before his notice was well in!
There was nothing surprising, of course, in the
fact that the women had already come to blows.
He had expected it, from the start, and, with the
resignation of custom, thought it as well over
soon as late. They had had one scrap, as it was,

from what Sarah had said, and the dregs of that pot of passion would still be hot enough to stir.

'It's a shame, that's what it is!' the girl was saying, over and over again. Tears dropped from the Geordie-an'-Jim eyes, and Simon felt furious with everybody, but particularly with himself.

'You needn't bother yourself,' he growled across at last, making a rough attempt to put the trouble right. 'Young Battersby's over much sense to go taking a spot like ourn, and as for his dad, he'll be back afore you can speak. 'Tisn't Sam Battersby, I'll be bound, if he isn't as pleased as punch to be running in double harness wi' Blindbeck and its brass!'

'Ay, like other folk!' Eliza dropped on him from the clouds, reappearing panting from her chase. 'Like other folk a deal nearer home, Simon Thornthet, as you don't need telling! Battersby wanted nowt wi' the farm—he tellt me so outside. 'Tisn't good enough for the likes of him, nor for our Emily Marion, neither! He was that stamping mad he was for breaking it all off, but I got him promised to look in again next week. I'd a deal o' work wi' him, all the same,' she added, flushing angrily at her brother-in-law's ironic smile, 'and no thanks to you, neither, if I come out top, after all! Anyway, I'll thank you to speak folk civilly at *my* table, if you can, whatever-like hired man's ways you keep for your own!'

She would have hectored him longer if Will had not got to his feet, and taken himself and his brother out of the room, so instead she went back to her seat and drank a large cup of tea in angry gulps. Between drinks, however, she managed

to say to the wife the things she had wanted to
say to the man, though Sarah was silent and paid
little or no heed. She wished she could have gone
outside with the men, and helped to decide what
her future was to be. But it was not for her to
advise, who would soon be no better than a helpless log. It was her part to wait patiently until
Simon fetched her away.

But it was not easy to wait at all in that atmosphere of critical dislike. The successive passages
of arms had had their natural effect, and the
party which had been so merry at the start was
now in a state of boredom and constraint. The
thoughts of most of those present were unfriendly
toward the folk of the marsh, and Sarah could
feel the thoughts winding about her in the air.
Emily Marion was right, so they were saying in
their minds; trouble always followed the Thornthwaites the moment they appeared. Storms
arose out of nowhere and destroyed some festive
occasion with a rush. Even to look at them,
dowdy and disapproving, was to take the heart
out of any happy day. It was certainly hard on
the poor Will Thornthwaites that the tiresome
Simons should dare to exist.

Sarah, bringing her mind back from the absent
brothers with an effort, found the Method working again at top speed. The tea had soothed
Eliza's nerves and stimulated her brain. She was
now at her very best for behaving her very worst.

'And so Mr. Addison's preaching next week, is
he?' she reverted suddenly, making even that
supreme egotist blink and start. Her voice, furred
and soft, reminded Sarah of a paw reaching out
for some one to scratch. 'Eh, now, but I should

be in a rare twitter if it was Will as was setting up
to preach! But there, we're none of us much of a
hand at talking, at our spot, and Will's summat
better to do than just wagging a loose tongue.
I'll see the lads come along, though, as it's you,
Mrs. Addison, and an old friend, unless there's
summat useful they're happen wanted for, at
home. Eh, Sarah, but wouldn't they talks to
young men ha' done a sight o' good to Geordie-
an'-Jim? It's a sad pity you didn't start preaching before they went, Mr. Addison—it is that!
Like enough, if you had, they'd be at Sandholes
yet.'

The preacher's brow had been thunderous
during the early part of this speech, but now he
looked suddenly coy. Sally, dropping her glance
to her aunt's lap, saw her fingers clench and
unclench on a fold of her old black gown.

'Any news of the prodigals?' Elliman Wilkinson suddenly inquired. He looked at Eliza as he
spoke, and smiled as at a well-known joke. 'I'm
always in hopes to find one of them eating the
fatted calf.'

'Nay, you must ask Sarah, not me!' Eliza
answered, with an affected laugh. She despised
Elliman in her heart, but she was grateful for the
cue. 'Sarah knows what they're at, if there's
anybody does at all. Like enough they'll turn up
one o' these days, but I don't know as we'll run
to calves. They'll be terble rough in their ways,
I doubt, after all this time. Out at elbows an' all,
as like as not, and wi' happen a toe or two keeking
through their boots!'

There was a ripple of laughter at this show of
wit, and then Elliman, urged by a nudge and a

whisper from Mary Phyllis, repeated the question in the proper quarter. He raised his voice when he spoke to Sarah, as if she were deaf as well as blind, and when she paused a moment before replying, he addressed her again. The whole table had pricked its ears and was listening by the time the answer came.

Sarah felt the giggles and the impertinent voice striking like arrows through the misty ring in which she sat. Sharpest of all was Eliza's laugh, introducing the question and afterwards punctuating it when it was put. She was achingly conscious of the antipathetic audience hanging on her lips. They were baiting her, and she knew it, and her heart swelled with helpless rage. A passionate longing seized her to be lord of them all for once—just for once to fling back an answer that would slay their smiles, put respect into their mocking voices and change their sneers into awed surprise. If only for once the dream and the glory might be true—the trap and the new clothes and Geordie and the green front-door! But nothing could be farther from what they expected, as she knew too well. They were waiting merely to hear her say what she had often said before—for news that there was no news or news that was worse than none. She had faced more than one trial, that day, and had come out of them with her self-respect intact, but this unexpected humiliation was more than she could bear. She was telling herself in the pause that she would not answer at all, when something that she took for the total revolt of pride spoke to the mockers through her lips.

'Ay, but there's rare good news!' she heard

herself saying in a cheerful tone, and instantly
felt her courage spring up and her heart lighten
as the lie took shape. 'I'd been saving it up,
Eliza, for when we were by ourselves, but there's
no sense, I reckon, in not saying it straight out.
Geordie's on his way home to England at this
very minute, and he says he's a rare good lining
to his jacket an' all!'

The air changed about her at once as she had
always dreamed it would, and she heard the gasp
of surprise pass from one to another like a quick-
thrown ball. Eliza started so violently that she
upset her cup and let it lie. She stared male-
volently at the other's face, her own set suddenly
into heavy lines.

'Nay, but that's news and no mistake!' she
exclaimed, striving after her former tone, but
without success. The note in her voice was clear
to her blind hearer, sending triumphant shivers
through her nerves. . . . 'Tell us again, will you,
Sarah!' she added sharply. 'I doubt I heard you
wrong.'

'I'll tell you and welcome till the cows come
home!' Sarah said, with a sudden sprightliness
that made the Wilkinson cousin open his eyes.
It was almost as if another person had suddenly
taken possession of Sarah's place. There was a
vitality about her that seemed to change her in
every feature, an easy dignity that transformed
the shabbiest detail of her dress. Her voice,
especially, had changed—that grudging, dully-
defiant voice. This was the warm, human voice
of one who rejoiced in secret knowledge, and
possessed her soul in perfect security and content.

'He's coming, I tell you—our Geordie's coming

back!' The wonderful words seemed to fill her with strong courage every time she spoke. 'I can't rightly tell you when it'll be, but he said we could look for him any minute now. Likely we'll find him waiting at Sandholes when we've gitten home. He's done well an' all, from what he says. . . . I'll be bound he's a rich man. He talks o' buying Sandholes, happen—or happen a bigger spot. I make no doubt he's as much brass as'd buy Blindbeck out an' out!'

She fell silent again after this comprehensive statement, merely returning brief ayes and noes to the questions showered upon her from every side. Her air of smiling dignity, however, remained intact, and even her blind eyes, moving from one to another eager face, impressed her audience with a sense of truth. And then above the excited chatter there rose Eliza's voice, with the mother-note sounding faintly through the jealous greed.

'Yon's all very fine and large, Sarah, but what about my Jim? Jim's made his pile an' all, I reckon, if Geordie's struck it rich. He's as smart as Geordie, is our Jim, any day o' the week! Hark ye, Sarah! What about my Jim?'

Quite suddenly Sarah began to tremble, exactly as if the other had struck her a sharp blow. She shrank instantly in her chair, losing at once her dignity and ease. The fine wine of vitality ran out of her as out of a crushed grape, leaving only an empty skin for any malignant foot to stamp into the earth. She tried to speak, but could find no voice brave enough to meet the fierce rain of Eliza's words. A mist other than that of blindness came over her eyes, and with a lost move-ment she put out a groping, shaking hand. Sally,

in a sudden access of pity, gathered it in her
own.

She slid her arm round her aunt, and drew her,
tottering and trembling, to her feet.

'It's over-much for her, that's what it is,' she
said kindly, but taking care to avoid her mother's
angry glance. 'It's knocked her over, coming
that sudden, and no wonder, either. Come along,
Aunt Sarah, and sit down for a few minutes in
the parlour. You'll be as right as a bobbin after
you've had a rest.'

She led her to the door, a lithe, upright figure
supporting trembling age, and Elliman's eyes
followed her, so that for once he was heedless of
Mary Phyllis when she spoke. Most of the company, indeed, had fallen into a waiting silence,
as if they knew that the act was not yet finished,
and that the cue for the curtain still remained to
be said. And the instinct that held them breathless was perfectly sound, for in the square of the
door Sarah halted herself and turned. Her worn
hands gripped her gown on either side, and if
May had been there to see her, she would again
have had her impression of shrouded flame. She
paused for a moment just to be sure of her breath,
and then her voice went straight with her blind
glance to the point where Eliza sat.

'Jim's dead, I reckon!' she said, clearly and
cruelly . . . 'ay, I doubt he's dead. Geordie'd
never be coming without him if he was over sod.
You'd best make up your mind, Eliza, as he's
dead and gone!'

It was the voice of an oracle marking an open
grave, of Cassandra, crying her knowledge in
Troy streets. It held them all spellbound until

she had gone out. Even Eliza was silent for once
on her red plush chair. . . .

IV

EACH of the brothers Thornthwaite drew a breath
of relief as soon as he got outside. They were at
ease together at once as soon as they were alone.
The contrast in their positions, so obvious to the
world, made little or no difference to the men
themselves. It would have made less still but for
the ever-recurring problem of the women-folk,
and even that they did their best to put away
from them as soon as they were out of sight. Each
could only plead what he could for the side he
was bound to support, and pass on hurriedly to
a less delicate theme. Alone they fell back easily
into the relation which had been between them
as lads, and forgot that the younger was now a
man of substance and weight, while the elder
had made an inordinate muddle of things. Will
had always looked up to Simon and taken his
word in much, and he still continued to take
it when Eliza was not present to point to the
fact that Simon's wonderful knowledge had not
worked out in practice. To-day, as they wandered
round the shippons, he listened respectfully while
his brother criticised the herd, quarrelled with
the quality of the food-stuffs, and snorted contempt at the new American method of tying
cattle in the stall. Experience had taught him
that Simon was not the first who had made a
mess of his own affairs while remaining perfectly
competent to hand out good advice to others.
The well-arranged water-supply was Simon's
idea, as well as the porcelain troughs which were

so easy to keep clean, and the milking-machine which saved so much in labour. There were other innovations—some, Eliza's pride—which were due to Simon, if only she had known it. He was a good judge of a beast, as well, and had a special faculty for doctoring stock, a gift which had certainly not been allowed to run to waste during those bewitched and disease-ridden years at Sandholes. Will was indebted to him for many valuable lives, and often said that Simon had saved him considerably more than he had ever lent him. It remained a perpetual mystery why so useful a man should have achieved so much for others and so little for himself. The answer could only lie in the curse that was glooming over Sandholes—if there was a curse. Nature certainly plays strange tricks on those who do not exactly suit her book, but in any case the hate at the heart of things was enough to poison luck at the very source.

While Sarah sat through her long torment in the kitchen, rising up at last for that great blow which at all events felled her adversary for the time being, Simon was enjoying himself airing his knowledge in the buildings, contradicting his brother on every possible occasion, and ending by feeling as if he actually owned the place. However, the reason of his visit came up at length, as it was bound to do, and his air of expert authority vanished as the position changed. One by one, as he had already done to Mr. Dent, he laid before his brother his difficulties and disappointments, much as a housewife lays out the chickens that some weasel has slain in the night. He wore the same air of disgust at such absurd

accumulation of disaster, of incredulity at this
overdone effort on the part of an inartistic fate.
The story was not new to Will, any more than to
the agent, but he listened to it patiently, nevertheless. He knew from experience that, unless
you allow a man to recapitulate his woes, you
cannot get him to the point from which a new
effort may be made. He may seem to be following
you along the fresh path which you are marking
out, but in reality he will be looking back at
the missed milestones of the past. And there were
so many, in Simon's case—so many behind him,
and so few to come. After all, it could be only
a short road and a bare into which even the
kindest brotherly love had power to set his feet.

So for the second time that day Simon lived
his long chapter of accidents over again; his voice,
by turns emphatic and indignant or monotonous
and resigned, falling like slanting rain over the
unheeding audience of the cattle. Will, listening
and nodding and revolving the question of ways
and means, had yet always a slice of attention
for his immediate belongings. His eye, casual yet
never careless, wandered over the warm roan
and ruddy and creamy backs between the clean
stone slabs which Simon had advocated in place
of the ancient wooden stalls. The herd was
indoors for the winter, but had not yet lost its
summer freshness, and he had sufficient cause
for pride in the straight-backed, clean-horned
stuff, with its obvious gentle breeding and beautiful, feminine lines. That part of his mind not
given to his brother was running over a string of
names, seeing in every animal a host of others
whose characteristics had gone to its creation,

and building upon them the stuff of the generations still to come—turning over, in fact, that store of knowledge of past history and patient prophecy for the future which gives the study of breeding at once its dignity and its fascination. At the far end of the shippon, where the calf-pens were, he could see the soft bundles of calves, with soft eyes and twitching ears, in which always the last word in the faith of the stock-breeder was being either proved or forsworn. The daylight, still dropping through skylights and windows, seemed to enter through frosted glass, dimmed as it was by the warm cloud of breathing as well as the mist that lined the sky beyond. A bird flew in at intervals through the flung-back swinging panes, and perched for a bar of song on the big cross-beams supporting the pointed roof. A robin walked pertly but daintily down the central aisle, a brave little spot of colour on the concrete grey, pecking as it went at the scattered corn under the monster-noses thrust between the rails. Simon leaned against a somnolent white cow, with an arm flung lengthways down her back, his other hand fretting the ground with the worn remnant of a crooked stick. Will's dog, a bushy, silvered thing, whose every strong grey hair seemed separately alive, curled himself, with an eye on the robin, at his master's feet.

The latter roused himself to greater attention when Simon reached the account of his interview with Mr. Dent. Accustomed as he was to more or less traditional behaviour in the traditional circumstances which govern such lives as his, he fastened at once on the puzzling attitude of the agent.

'It fair beats me what Mr. Dent could think he
was at,' he observed thoughtfully. 'Once you'd
settled to quit there was no sense in keeping you
hanging on. Best make a job and ha' done wi' it,
seems to me. 'Tisn't like Mr. Dent, neither, to
carry on in such a fashion. I wonder what made
him act so strange?'

Simon wore his original air of injured dignity
as he leaned against the cow.

'Nay, I don't know, I'm sure, but he was terble
queer! You might ha' thought he was badly or
summat, but he seemed all right. Come to that,
he looked as fit as a fiddle and as pleased as
a punch! You might ha' thought he'd had a
fortune left him, or the King's crown!'

'Happen it was some private business,' Will
said, 'and nowt to do wi' you at all. . . . What
did you think o' doing when you've quit the
farm?'

Simon poked the flags harder than ever, and
from injured dignity sank to sulks. The sudden
pressure of his arm moved the somnolent cow to
a sharp kick. When he spoke, it was in a surly
tone, and with his eyes turned away from Will's.

'I'll have to get a job o' some sort, I reckon, to
keep us going. I'm over old for most folk, but I
could happen do odds and ends—fetching milk
and siding up, and a bit o' gardening and such-
like. The trouble is the missis won't be able to do
for herself before so long. The doctor tellt her
to-day she was going blind.'

His brother's face filled at once with sympathy
and dismay. In that forbidden compartment of
his mind where he sometimes ventured to criticise
his wife, he saw in a flash how she would take the

news. This latest trouble of Sarah's would indeed be the summit of Eliza's triumph. Poverty Sarah had withstood; blindness she might have mastered, given time; but poverty and blindness combined would deliver her finally into the enemy's hand.

'I never thought it would be as bad as that,' he murmured pityingly. 'It's a bad business, is that! . . . Didn't doctor say there was anything could be done?'

'There was summat about an operation, but it'll get no forrarder,' Simon said. 'They fancy things is hardly in Sarah's line.'

'If it's brass that's wanted, you needn't fash over that. . . .' He added more urgently as Simon shook his head, 'It'd be queer if I grudged you brass for a thing like yon!'

'You're right kind,' Simon said gratefully, 'but it isn't no use. She's that proud, is Sarah, she'll never agree. I doubt she just means to let things slide.'

'She's no call, I'm sure, to be proud with me!' Will's voice was almost hot. 'I've always been ready any time to stand her friend. Anyway, there's the offer, and she can take it or leave it as best suits her. If she changes her mind after a while, she won't find as I've altered mine. . . . But there's no sense in your taking a job and leaving a blind woman to fend for herself. There's nowt for it but Sarah'll have to come to us.'

Simon laughed when he said that, a grim, mirthless laugh which made the dog open his sleepless eyes and throw him a searching glance.

'Nay, nay, Will, my lad! It's right good of you, but it wouldn't do. A bonny time you'd have, to be sure, wi' the pair on 'em in t'house!

And anyway your missis'd never hear tell o' such a thing, so that fixes it right off.'

'It's my own spot, I reckon!' Will spoke with unusual force. 'I can do as suits me, I suppose. T'lasses hasn't that much to do they can't see to a blind body, and as for room and such-like, there'll be plenty, soon. Young Battersby's made it up with our Em, and it's more than time yon Elliman Wilkinson was thinking o' getting wed. He's been going with our Sally a terble long while, though he and Mary Phyllis seem mighty throng, just now. Anyway, there'll be a corner for Sarah right enough—ay, and for you an' all.'

But Simon shook his head again, and stood up straight and took his arm off the back of the cow.

'There'd be murder, I doubt,' he said quite simply, and this time he did not laugh. 'There's bad blood between they two women as nobbut death'll cure. Nay, I thank ye right enough, Will, but yon horse won't pull. . . .

'I mun get a job, that's all,' he went on quickly, before Will could speak again, 'and some sort of a spot where t'neighbours'll look to the missis while I'm off. I'll see t'agent agen and try to ram into him as I mean to gang, and if you hear of owt going to suit, you'll likely let me know?'

Will nodded, but did not answer because of approaching steps, and they stood silently waiting until the cowman showed at the door. At once, the deep symphony of the hungry broke from the cattle at sight of their servant with his swill. The quiet picture, almost as still as if painted on the wall, upheaved suddenly into a chaos of rocking, bellowing beasts. The great heads tugged at their yokes, the great eyes pleaded and rolled.

The big organ-notes of complaint and desire chorded and jarred, dropping into satisfied silence as the man passed from stall to stall. Will jerked his head after him as he went out at the far door, and said that he would be leaving before so long.

'Eh? Taylor, did ye say?' Simon stared, for the man had been at Blindbeck for years. 'What's amiss?'

'Nay, there's nowt wrong between us, if you mean that. But his wife's father's had a stroke, and wants him to take over for him at Drigg. News didn't come till I was off, this morning, or I might ha' looked round for somebody while I was in t'town.'

Simon began a fresh violent poking with his ancient stick. 'You'll ha' somebody in your eye, likely?' he enquired. 'There'll be plenty glad o' the job.'

'Oh, ay, but it's nobbut a weary business learning folk your ways.' He glanced at his brother a moment, and then looked shyly away. 'If you're really after a shop, Simon, what's wrong wi' it for yourself?'

The painful colour came into the other's averted face. He poked so recklessly that he poked the dog, who arose with an offended growl.

'Nay, it's charity, that's what it is! I'm over old. . . . You know as well as me I'd never get such a spot anywheres else.'

'You know the place, and you're a rare hand wi' stock. I could trust you same as I could myself.'

'I'm over old,' Simon demurred again, 'and done, to boot. I'd not be worth the brass.'

'We've plenty o' help on the place,' Will said.

'It'd be worth it, just to have you about. Nigh the same as having a vet on t'spot!' he added jokingly, trying to flatter him into acquiescence. 'I'd be main glad, for my own sake,' he went on, his face grave again and slightly wistful. 'There's times I fair ache for a crack wi' somebody o' my own. Women is nobbut women, when all's said and done, and lads is like to think they know a deal better than their dad. . . . Ay, well, you can think it over and let me know,' he finished, in a disappointed tone.

Simon poked for a while longer, and succeeded in poking the cow as well as the dog. He was fighting hard with his pride as he scraped busily at the flags. The tie of blood pulled him, as well as the whole atmosphere of the prosperous place. He knew in his heart that he was never so happy as when he was with his brother, never so good a man as when he was preaching in Will's shippons. As for pride, that would have to go by the board, sooner or later; indeed, who would say that he had any right to it, even now? He made up his mind at last on a sudden impulse, lifting his head with a hasty jerk.

'I've had enough o' thinking things over, thank ye all the same. I'll be main glad o' the job, Will, and that's the truth. . . .' He sank back instantly, however, and fell to poking again. 'Folk'll have plenty to say, though, I reckon,' he added bitterly, 'when they hear as I'm hired man to my younger brother!'

'They've always a deal to say, so what's the odds? As for younger and older, there isn't a deal to that when you get up in years. . . . There's a good cottage across t'road,' he went on eagerly, bringing up reinforcements before Simon should retire. 'It's handy for t'stock, and there's a garden and orchard as well. Lasses could see to Sarah, you'll think on, if she's that close. There's berry-bushes in t'garden and a deal besides. . . .'

Simon was busy shaking his head and saying he wasn't worth it and that he was over old, but all the time he was listening with interest and even pleasure to Will's talk. Milking had now begun, and already, as the levers swung back and forwards over the cattle's heads, he found himself looking about the shippon with a possessive eye. Even in these few moments, life had taken a turn for the Thornthwaite of the desolate marsh farm. Already his back felt stronger, his eye brighter, his brain more alive. The drawbacks of the proposed position began to recede before the many advantages it had to offer. It was true, of course, that he would be his brother's hired man, but it was equally true that he was the master's brother, too. To all intents and purposes he would be master himself—that is to say, when Eliza wasn't about! Will's cottages were good, like everything else of Will's, and the lasses could see to Sarah, as he said. For himself there would be the constant interest and stimulant of a big farm, as well as the mental relief of a steady weekly wage. He felt almost excited about it as they crossed the yard, making for Taylor's cottage over the road. He tried not to think of what Sarah might say when she heard the news, still less of what Mrs. Will would most certainly say. He felt equal to both of them in his present spirited mood, and even tried to convince himself that in time they would make friends.

As they stood looking at Taylor's cottage and Taylor's gooseberry bushes and canes, Will suddenly asked his brother whether there was any news of Geordie. And Simon, when he had given the old answer that there was no news that was worth crossing the road to hear, turned his face away in the direction of Taylor's hens, and enquired whether there was any news of Jim.

'There's been none for a sight o' years now,' Will answered sadly, leaning on the wall. 'Eliza wrote him a letter as put his back up, and he's never sent us a line since. He always set a deal more by you and your missis than he ever did by us. I'd ha' stood his friend, poor lad, if he'd ha' let me, but he always took it I was agen him, too.'

There was silence between them for a while, and then—'Eh, well, you've a mort of others to fill his place!' Simon sighed, watching a well-built lad swing whistling across the yard.

Will raised himself from the wall, and watched him, too.

'Ay, but I'd nobbut the one eldest son!' was all he said.

V

SALLY led her aunt to the grand but unused parlour in which so many expensive and handsome things were doomed to spend their lives. There was a piano, of course, which none of the Blindbeck folk knew how to play, in spite of Eliza's conviction that the gift was included in the price. A Chippendale bookcase made a prison for strange books never opened and never named, and the shut doors of a cabinet kept watch and ward over some lovely china and glass. There was a satin-wood table with a velvet sheen, a polished mirror which never reflected a laughing human face. There was an American rocking-chair, poised like a floating bird, with cushions filled with the finest down ever drawn from an heirloom of a feather-bed. Sarah would not have taken the rocking-chair, as a rule; she would have thought herself either too humble or too proud. But to-day she went to it as a matter of course, because of the false pomp that she had drawn to herself like a stolen royal robe. With a sigh of relief that was half physical and half mental, she let herself gently down, dropped her rusty bonnet against the silk, and peacefully closed her eyes.

Sally stood looking at her with an expression of mingled pity, curiosity, and awe. She had pitied her often enough before, but she had never before seen her through the slightest veil of romance. Sometimes, indeed, the tale of the damaged wedding-day had touched her imagination like the scent of a bruised flower, but it was so faint and far-off that it passed again like a breath. To-day, however, she had that sudden sense of exquisite beauty in the old, which all must feel who see in them the fragile storehouses of life. The old woman had known so much that she would never know, looked on a different world with utterly different eyes. There was romance in the thought of the dead she had seen and spoken to and laughed with and touched and loved. And even now, with the flower of her life apparently over and withered back again to its earth, this sudden splendour of Geordie had blossomed for her at the end.

The girl waited a moment, hoping for a word, and then, though rather reluctantly, turned towards the door. She wanted to hear still more about the marvellous news, but the old woman looked so tired that she did not like to ask. She was anxious, too, to get back to the kitchen to keep an eye on Mary Phyllis. Yet still she lingered, puzzled and curious, and still touched by that unusual sense of awe. An exotic beauty had passed swiftly into the musty air of Eliza's parlour, a sense of wonder from worlds beyond . . . the strong power of a dream.

'You're over-tired, aren't you, Aunt Sarah?' she repeated, for want of something better to say. She spoke rather timidly, as if aware that the words only brushed the surface of deeper things below.

Sarah answered her without opening her eyes.

'Ay, my lass. Just a bit.'

'You'd best stop here quietly till Uncle Simon's yoked up. I'll see nobody bothers you if you feel like a nap. I'd fetch you a drop of cowslip wine, but mother's got the key.'

'Nay, I want nowt wi' it, thank ye,' Sarah said. 'I'll do all right.' She lifted her hands contentedly and folded them in her lap. 'Likely I'll drop off for a minute, as you say.'

'Ay, well, then, I'd best be getting back.' She moved resolutely now, but paused with her hand on the latch. 'Aunt Sarah,' she asked rather breathlessly, 'was all that about Cousin Geordie *true*?'

Sarah's lids quivered a little, and then tightened over her eyes.

'Ay. True enough.'

'It's grand news, if it is! . . . I'm right glad about it, I'm sure! I've always thought it hard

lines, him going off like that. And you said he'd
done well for himself, didn't you, Aunt Sarah? ...
Eh, but I wish Elliman could make some brass
an' all!'

'There's a deal o' power in brass.' The words
came as if of themselves from behind the mask-
like face. 'Folks say it don't mean happiness,
but it means power. It's a stick to beat other
folk wi', if it's nowt else.'

'I don't want to beat anybody, I'm sure!' Sally
laughed, though with tears in her voice. 'I only
want what's my own.'

'Ay, we all on us want that,' Sarah said, with
a grim smile. 'But it's only another fancy name
for the whole world!'

.   .   .   .   .

She sat still for some time after the girl had
gone out, as if she were afraid that she might
betray herself before she was actually alone.
Presently, however, she began to rock gently to
and fro, still keeping her hands folded and her
eyes closed. The good chair moved easily without creak or jar, and the good cushions adapted
themselves to every demand of her weary bones.
Geordie should buy her a chair like this, she
told herself as she rocked, still maintaining the
wonderful fiction even to herself. She would
have cushions, too, of the very best, covered with
silk, and cool to a tired cheek. A footstool, also,
ample and well stuffed, and exactly the right
height for a pair of aching feet.

But though one half of her brain continued to
dally with these pleasant fancies, the other was
standing amazed before her late stupendous act.
She was half-aghast, half-proud at the ease with

which she had suddenly flung forth her swift, gigantic lie. Never for a moment had she intended to affirm anything of the kind; never as much as imagined that she might hint at it even in joke. She had been angry, of course, bitter and deeply hurt, but there had been no racing thoughts in her mind eager to frame the princely tale. It had seemed vacant, indeed, paralysed by rage, unable to do little else but suffer and hate. And then suddenly the words had been said, had shaped themselves on her lips and taken flight, as if by an agency with which she had nothing to do. It was just as if somebody had taken her arm and used it to wave a banner in the enemy's face; as if she were merely an instrument on which an angry hand had suddenly played.

So she was not ashamed, or even really alarmed, because of this inward conviction that the crime was not her own. Yet the voice had been hers, and most certainly the succeeding grim satisfaction and ironic joy had been hers! She allowed herself an occasional chuckle, now that she was really alone, gloating freely over Eliza's abasement and acute dismay. For once at least, in the tourney of years, she had come away victor from the fray. No matter how she was made to pay for it, in the end, she had had the whip hand of Blindbeck just for once. Indeed, now that it was done—and so easily done—she marvelled that she had never done it before. At the back of her mind, however, was the vague knowledge that there is only one possible moment for tremendous happenings such as these. Perhaps the longing engendered by the dream in the yard had suddenly grown strong enough to act of its own

accord. Perhaps, as in the decision about the
farm, a sentence lying long in the brain is spoken
at length without the apparent assistance of the
brain. . . .

She did not trouble herself even to speculate
how she would feel when at last the truth was out.
This was the truth, as long as she chose to keep it
so, as long as she sat and rocked and shut the
world from her dreaming eyes. From pretending
that it was true she came very soon to believing
that it might really be possible, after all. Such
things had happened more than once, she knew,
and who was to say that they were not happening
now? She told herself that, if she could believe
it with every part of herself just for a moment, it
would be true. Up in heaven, where, as they
said, a star winked every time a child was born,
they had only to move some lever or other, and
it would be true.

A clock ticked on the mantelpiece with a slow,
rather hesitating sound, as if trying to warn the
house that Sunday and the need of the winding-
key were near. There was a close, secretive
feeling in the room, the atmosphere of so many
objects shut together in an almost terrible proxi-
mity for so many days of the week. She was so
weary that she could have fallen asleep, but her
brain was too much excited to let her rest. The
magnitude of her crime still held her breathlessly
enthralled; the glamour of it made possible all
impossible hopes. She dwelt again and again on
the spontaneity of the lie, which seemed to give
it the unmistakable stamp of truth.

She had long since forgotten what it was like to
be really happy or even at peace, but in some

sort of fierce, gloating, heathenish way she was
happy now. She was conscious, for instance, of
a sense of importance beyond anything she had
ever known. Even that half of her brain which
insisted that the whole thing was pretence could
not really chill the pervading glow of pride. She
had caught the reflection of her state in Eliza's
voice, as well as in others less familiar to her ear.
She had read it even in Sally's kindly champion-
ship and support; through the sympathy she had
not failed to hear the awe. The best proof—if
she needed proof—was that she was actually here
in the sacred parlour, and seated in the precious
chair. Eliza would have turned her out of both,
long since, she knew, if she had not been clad in
that new importance as in cloth of gold.

The impossible lies nearer than mere proba-
bility to the actual fact; so near, at times, that
the merest effort seems needed to cross the line.
Desire, racking both soul and body with such
powerful hands, must surely be strong enough
to leap the slender pale. The peculiar mockery
about ill-luck is always the trifling difference
between the opposite sides of the shield. It is the
difference between the full glass and the glass
turned upside-down. But to-day at least this
tired old woman had swung the buckler round,
and laughed as she held the glass in her hand and
saw the light strike through the wine.

In this long day of Simon's and Sarah's nothing
was stranger than the varying strata of glamour
and gloom through which in turn they passed.
Their days and weeks were, as a rule, mere grey
blocks of blank, monotonous life, imperceptibly
lightened or further shadowed by the subtle

changes of the sky. But into these few hours so closely packed with dreadful humiliations and decisions, so much accumulated unkindness and insult and cold hate, there kept streaming upon them shafts of light from some centre quite unknown. For Simon there had been the unexpected stimulant of his Witham success, and, later, the new interest in life which Will's proposal had seemed to offer. For Sarah there was the wistful pleasure of her morning with May, as well as the unlawful but passionate pleasure of her present position. The speed of the changes kept them overstrung, so that each as it came found them more sensitive than the last. They were like falling bodies dropping by turn through cloud and sunlit air. They were like total wrecks on some darkened sea, catching and losing by turn the lights of an approaching vessel.

The slow clock dragged the protesting minutes on, and still no one disturbed her, and the dream widened and grew. Tea would be brought in, soon, she told herself, in the dream—strong, expensive, visitor's tea, freshly boiled and brewed. The silver teapot would be queening it over the tray, flanked by steaming scones and an oven-new, home-made cake. Eliza herself would appear to entertain her guest, always with that new note of reverence in her voice. When the door opened, they would hear another voice—Geordie's, laughing and talking in some room beyond. All the happy young voices of the house would mingle with his, but always the youngest and happiest would be Geordie's own. Hearing that voice, she would make mock of herself for ever having feared Eliza's tongue; still more

for ever having cared enough to honour her with
hate. A small thing then would be the great
Eliza, in spite of her size, beside the mother for
whom the dead had been made alive. She would
talk with Eliza as the gods talk when they speak
with the humble human from invisible heights.
So strong was the vision that she found herself
framing the godlike sentences with gracious ease.
The silver teaspoons clinked against the cups,
and the visitor's tea was fragrant in the musty
room. She spread a linen handkerchief across
her knee . . . a snowy softness against her silken
knee. . . . And always, always, as the meal pro-
gressed, the voice of her ecstasy sang in her happy
ear. . . .

She had that one moment of clear beauty
unprofaned by hate, with Geordie's face swimming before her in a golden haze. Then her
hand, going out to the silk and linen of the dream,
encountered the darned and threadbare serge of
dreary fact. The dream rent violently all around
her, letting her out again into the unlovely
world. Even her blindness had been forgotten,
for the time, for in the dream she was never blind.
Now the touch of the darns under her hand
brought back the long hours of mending by candlelight which had had their share in despoiling her
of her sight. She would never be able to darn
by candlelight again, and the loss of that drudgery
seemed to her now an added grief, because into
this and all similar work, as women know, goes
the hope of the future to emerge again as the soul
of the past. . . . Sarah knew that her hand would
ache for her needle as the sailor's hand aches
for the helm, or the crippled horseman's for

the feel of the flat rein. She felt, too, a sudden desperate anger against the woman who would have the mending of Simon's clothes. Geordie's, she knew, she would simply have wrenched from any stranger's hands, but, since there was no Geordie, she need not think of that. The dream had been merely the make-believe of the bitterly oppressed, who had taken to desperate lying as a last resort. Yet still the sweetness lingered, keeping her serene, like the last scent of a passed garden or the last light upon darkening hills.

She smoothed her hands on the arms of the precious chair, and reached out and smoothed the satin of the table. Through the dimness the solid piano loomed, the rosewood coffin of a thousand songs. The carpet under her feet felt elastic yet softly deep. There were ornaments in the room, good stuff as well as trash; trifles pointing the passions of Eliza's curious soul. But for once, after all these years, Eliza's soul would be sorrowful in spite of her great possessions. Back in the kitchen she would be gritting her teeth on the fact that it was Sarah's son who was coming home, coming with money to burn and a great and splendid will to burn it. She would exact payment, of course, when the truth was known, but even the last ounce of payment could not give her back this hour. For this hour, at least, it was hers to suffer and Sarah's to reign. For this hour, at least, the heavily-weighted tables of destiny were turned. . . .

VI

THAT which had been the terrible Eliza sat still for a long moment after Sarah had gone out.

There was silence about the table until Elliman Wilkinson took upon himself to speak.

'But Jim's never *your* son, Cousin Eliza?' he exclaimed, puzzled, rushing in where not only angels would have feared to tread, but where the opposite host also would have taken care to keep their distance. 'It's very stupid of me, of course, but I've always made sure that Geordie-an'-Jim were twins.'

Eliza turned baleful eyes upon the eager, inquisitive face. Her mind, concentrated in sullen fury upon the enemy recently departed with banners, found a difficulty in focussing itself upon this insignificant shape. When it succeeded, however, she ground him into dust.

'Ay, well, next time you feel sure of anything, you can make certain you're dead wrong!' she told him cruelly, surveying his bland countenance with cold contempt. 'Jim's my eldest, if you want to know, and as much the better o' Geordie as Blindbeck's the better o' yon mudhole down on the marsh! He was always the smarter lad o' the two—'tisn't likely he'd ha' been left. . . . I'll lay what you like it's Jim as is really coming, after all!'

'But in that case you would surely have heard from him yourself?' Elliman was still disporting himself with the brazen folly of innocence upon the forbidden ground. 'He'd have written to tell his mother, surely—not his aunt?'

A distinct thrill of apprehension ran through the company at this tactful speech. Mary Phyllis's nudge on this occasion was one of sharp reproof. The clouds thickened on Eliza's brow.

'Nay, then, he just wouldn't, Mr. Clever-Lad-

Know-All, so that's that! I'm his mother right
enough, as nobody but a fool would ha' needed
telling, but he wouldn't ha' written me, all the
same. Me and Jim got across, a while back, and
he's taken sulks with me, ever since. He'd be like
enough to write to Sarah, by way of giving me
back a bit o' my own. She always cockered him
fearful, did Sarah, and set him agen me when-
ever she could. And if there's brass about, as she
says, she'll keep it warm for him, never fear!
She'll take right good care it never gets past her
to Blindbeck or any of his own!'

'Jim would ha' been right enough but for
Geordie, all along.' Mrs. Addison shook a loose
and agile bonnet with an impressive air. 'He
was a right-down nuisance, was Geordie Thornthet—a bad lad as well as a reg'lar limb! Such
tricks as he was up to, I'm sure—turmut-lanterns
and the like, booin' at folks' winders after dark,
and hiding behind hedges when folk was courtin'
about t'lanes! Stephen and me wasn't wed then,
you'll think on, and I mind a terble fright as
Geordie give us, one summer night. Stephen
was terble sweet on me, as you'll likely know,
though he'd choke himself black in the face afore
he'd own to it now. Well, yon night as I'm
speaking of, he had hold o' my hand, and was
looking as near like a dying duck in a thunder-
storm as ever I see. "Jenny Sophia," he was
saying, as sweet as a field of clover, "I'm that set
on you, Jenny Sophia"—when up pops Geordie
on t'far side o' the hedge, girning and making a
hullaballoo like a donkey afore rain!'

'You've no call to go raking up yon d—d
rubbish!' Mr. Addison burst out, crimson to the

hair, and quite forgetting the obligations of his
Christian mission. He had said the same thing
to Eliza's eldest lass, and much about the same
time, and knew that Eliza knew it as well as he.
'Folks isn't right in their heads when they're
courtin', as everybody knows, and it's real mean
to bring it agen 'em, after all these years. As for
Geordie Thornthet, there was lile or nowt I could
learn *him*, and that's sure! T'lasses was always
after him like bees at a bottle o' rum.'

'Nay, now, you mean our Jim!' Jim's mother
corrected him with an air of offence. 'Nobody
never reckoned nowt o' Geordie but May Fleming. He couldn't hold a candle to Jim, any day
o' the week. Folk said they couldn't tell 'em
apart, but I never see a scrap o' likeness, myself.'
She glanced defiantly round the table, as if expect-
ing opposition, and then swung round eagerly as
Sally reappeared. 'Well, my lass, well?' she
rapped out—'did she tell you anything more?
You've taken your time about coming back, I'm
sure!'

'Nay, she said nowt fresh,' Sally answered
evasively, without meeting her eyes. She advanced to the table and began to gather the
china together, ready for clearing away. Her
mother pushed back her chair with an angry
scrape.

'Well, of all the gert, helpless gabies!' she
exploded violently. 'I made sure she'd talk when
she'd gitten you by herself. Didn't she say when
letter come, or how much brass there was, or
owt? . . . Eh, well, it's never Geordie as made
it, that I'll swear!'

'She said it was Geordie.' Sally went on

mechanically with her task, collecting cups and plates from under the noses of the still-stupefied clan. 'It's real nice, anyway, to see somebody happy,' she added suddenly, raising her eyes to look at the smug cousin. Elliman met them unexpectedly and coloured furiously. On a sudden remorseful impulse he shuffled a couple of plates together, and handed them to her with a deprecating air.

'I can't say she looked very set up about it, anyhow!' Eliza sneered. 'What, she was even more glumpy than usual, seemed to me!'

'More like a burying than a home-coming, by a deal!' Mary Phyllis finished for her, with a scornful laugh.

'As for Uncle Simon, he was as cross as a pair of shears!' Emily Marion added, in a fretted tone. The Thornthwaites were making things awkward to-day for the bride-to-be. Simon had nearly queered the engagement, at the start, and now the company's interest was all for a Thornthwaite whom she had never seen.

'Not how *I* should take good news, certainly!' Elliman said, hoping that no one had noticed his menial act. 'I should have something more to say for myself, I hope, than that.'

Eliza's eyes brightened considerably at this unanimous point of view.

'Nay, you're right there,' she took them up eagerly. 'You're right enough! 'Tisn't natural to be so quiet. I'll tell you what it is,' she added impressively, 'it's one o' two things, that's all. It's either a lie from beginning to end, or else— or else—well, it's our Jim!' She pushed her chair farther still, and got hurriedly to her feet.

'Ay, well, whichever it is, I'd best see for myself,' she added quickly. 'You'll not mind me leaving you, Mrs. Addison, just for a little while? I don't know as we're doing right to leave Sarah so long alone. She's getting a bit of an old body now, you know, and she was never that strong in her poor head.'

She departed noisily after this surprisingly sympathetic speech, and Sarah, hearing her heavy step along the passage, chuckled for the last time. Her mind braced itself for the coming contest with a grim excitement that was almost joy. Nothing could have been more unlike her attitude of the morning in the inn-yard. She lay back in her chair again and closed her eyes, and was rocking peacefully when Eliza opened the door.

Just for the moment the sight of the tranquil figure gave her pause, but neither sleep nor its greater counterpart could still Eliza for very long. 'Feeling more like yourself, are you, Sarah?' she enquired cautiously, peering in, and then repeated the question when she got no answer. Finally, irritated by the other's immobility which was obviously not sleep, she entered the room heavily, shutting the door with a sharp click. 'There's nowt amiss, from the look of you,' she added loudly, as she advanced.

Sarah exclaimed, 'Eh, now, whatever's yon!' at the sound of the harsh voice, and sat up stiffly, winking her blind eyes. She even turned her head and blinked behind, as if she thought the voice had come out of the grandfather's clock. 'Nay, I'll do now, thank ye,' she answered politely, discovering Eliza's whereabouts with a show of surprise. 'It'll be about time we were thinking of getting off.'

Eliza, however, had no intention of parting with her, just yet. She stopped her hastily when she tried to rise.

'Nay, now, there isn't that much hurry, is there?' she demanded sharply. 'Yon old horse o' yourn'll barely have stretched his legs. Your master and mine'd have a deal to say to each other an' all.' She paused a moment, creaking from foot to foot, and staring irresolutely at the mask-like face. 'You talked a deal o' stuff in t'other room, Sarah,' she broke out at last, 'but I reckon you meant nowt by it, after all?'

Sarah wanted to chuckle again, but was forced to deny herself the pleasure. For appearance' sake she stiffened her back, and bristled a little at Eliza's tone.

'Ay, but I did!' she retorted briskly, her voice firm. 'Whatever else should I mean, I'd like to know?'

The strong hope that had sprung in Eliza's heart died down again before this brazen show.

'You can't rightly know what you're saying, Sarah,' she said coldly, 'you can't, indeed! Geordie coming, after all these years—nay, now, yon isn't true!'

'Ay, but it is, I tell ye—true enough! True as yon Sunday fringe o' yourn as you bought in Witham!'

'And wi' brass, you said!' Eliza let the flippant remark pass without notice, and Sarah nodded. 'A deal o' brass!'

'Yon's what he says.'

'Eh, well, I never did!' The angry wind of

her sigh passed over Sarah's head and rustled
the honesty in a vase behind. She repeated 'I
never did!' and creaked away from the enemy
towards the window. Behind her, Geordie's
mother allowed the ghost of a smile to find a
fleeting resting-place on her lips.

'And so he's on his road home, is he—coming
right back?' Mrs. Will kept her back turned,
thinking hard as she spoke. There was no section
of Sarah's statement but she intended to prove
by the inch. 'Ay, well, it's what they mostly do
when they've made their brass.'

'He'll be over here, I reckon, afore you can say
knife! Taking first boat, he says he is, or the
fastest he can find.' She turned her head towards
the door through which his voice had come in
the dream. 'What, I shouldn't be that surprised
if he was to open yon door now!'

There was such conviction in her tone that
Eliza, too, was startled into turning her head.
There was nothing to see, of course, and she
turned back, but her ears still thrilled with the
thrill in Sarah's voice. The cowman, passing,
saw her face behind the glass, and said to himself that the missis was out for trouble once
again.

She was silent for a while, trying vainly to
grapple the situation in the pause. She saw well
enough that there was nothing to be gained by
dispute if the story were true. She still looked to
be top-dog in that or any other case, because
Blindbeck pride was founded on solid Blindbeck
gold; but there was no denying that the enemy
would be in a totally different position, and
would have to be met on totally different ground.

If, on the other hand, the great statement was a lie, there would be plenty of time for vengeance when the facts were known. Her malicious soul argued that the real game was to give Sarah plenty of rope, but her evil temper stood in the way of the more subtle method. It got the upper hand of her, at last, and she flung round with an angry swing.

'Nay, then, I can't believe it!' she exclaimed passionately—'I just can't! It's a pack o' lies, that's what it is, Sarah—a gert string o' senseless lies!'

This coarse description of her effort hurt Sarah in her artistic pride. She stiffened still further.

'I reckoned you'd take it like that,' she replied in a dignified tone. ''Tisn't decent nor Christian, but it's terble nat'ral.'

'I don't see how you could look for folks to take it different!' Eliza cried. ''Tisn't a likely sort o' story, any way round. Ne'er-do-weels don't make their fortunes every day o' the week, and your Geordie was a wastrel, if ever there was one, yet. You don't look like good news, neither, come to that. They've just been saying so in t'other room.'

'Good news wants a bit o' getting used to,' Sarah said quietly, 'same as everything else. When you've never had no luck for years and years, you don't seem at first as if you could rightly take it in.'

'More particular when you're making it up out o' your own head!' Eliza scoffed, but growing more and more unwillingly convinced. 'Nay, now, Sarah!' she added impatiently, her hands twitching—'what d'ye think ye're at? What

about all yon talk o' giving up the farm? No
need for such a to-do if Geordie's coming
home!'

For the first time, though only just for a second,
Sarah quailed. For the first time she had a
glimpse of the maze in which she had set her feet,
and longed sharply for her physical sight as if it
would help her mental vision. But her brain was
still quick with the power of the dream, and it
rose easily to the sudden need. 'It's like this, d'ye
see,' she announced firmly. 'Simon knows nowt
about it yet. I didn't mean telling him till we'd
gitten back.'

Eliza had followed the explanation with lower-
ing brows, but now she burst into one of her
great laughs.

'Losh, Sarah, woman! but I'd have a better
tale than that! What, you'd never ha' let him
give in his notice, and you wi' your tongue in
your cheek all the time! . . . When did you get
yon precious letter o' yours?' she enquired swiftly,
switching on to another track.

'Just last minute this morning as we was starting off.' Sarah was thoroughly launched now on
her wild career. Each detail as she required it
rose triumphantly to her lips. 'Simon was back
in t'stable wi' t'horse when postman come, so I
put it away in my pocket and settled to say nowt.
I thought it was likely axing for money or summat
like that, and Simon had more than enough to
bother him, as it was. I got May Fleming to read
it for me at doctor's,' she finished simply, with a
supreme touch. 'I'm terble bad wi' my eyes,
Eliza, if you'll trouble to think on.'

Once again Eliza was forced to belief against

her will, and then once again she leaped at the only discrepancy in the tale.

'You could ha' tellt Simon easy enough on the road out!' she threw at her in a swift taunt. 'There's time for a deal o' telling at *your* rate o' speed!'

But now, to her vexed surprise, it was Sarah who laughed, and with a society smoothness that would have been hard to beat. It was in matters like these that the dream lifted her into another sphere, puzzling her clumsy antagonist by the finer air she seemed to breathe.

'Eh, now, Eliza!' she said good-humouredly, and with something almost like kindliness in her voice, 'whatever-like use is it telling a man owt when he's chock full o' summat else? Simon was fit to crack himself over some joke as he'd heard in Witham, talking a deal o' nonsense and laughing fit to shake the trap! Coming from market's no time any day for telling a man important news, and anyway I'd never ha' got a word in edgeways if I'd tried.' She paused a moment, and then continued, aspiring to still greater heights. 'I'd another reason an' all for wanting it kept quiet. I knew he'd be sure an' certain to go shouting it out here.'

'Ay, and why ever not, I'd like to know!' Eliza gasped, when she was able to speak. 'Come to that, you were smart enough shoving it down our throats yourself!'

'Ay, but that was because I lost my temper,' Sarah admitted, with a noble simplicity which again struck the other dumb. 'If I hadn't ha' lost my temper,' she added, 'I should ha' said nowt—*nowt*!'—a statement so perfectly true in itself that it needed nothing to make it tell. 'I never meant you should hear it so sudden-like,' she went on gently, the kindness growing in her voice. 'It's hard lines our Geordie should ha' done so well for himself, and not your Jim. I never meant to crow over you about it, Eliza— I didn't, indeed. I never thought o' such a thing!'

Eliza was making a noise like a motor-car trying to start, but Sarah took up her tale before she could reply.

'As for letting Simon give in his notice as we'd fixed, I don't know as it'll make that much differ, after all. There's my eyes, for one thing, as I mentioned before. Blind folk are only a nuisance wherever they be, but they're a real, right-down nuisance on a farm. And Geordie'll want more nor a farm, I reckon, wi' all yon brass to splash. He'll want summat wi' stables and gardens and happen fishing an' all—a grand gentleman's spot, likely, same as the Hall itself.'

Mrs. Will felt the world wheeling rapidly about her, and tried to clutch at it as it went. Her temples throbbed and her throat worked, and her staring eyes went blind. She groped her way to the window, and flung up the stiff sash; and, as she stood there, drawing panting breaths, Simon and Will came sauntering through the yard. Her eyes, clearing again in the rush of air, caught the incipient smile on Simon's face, the new signs of interest and life in his whole look. He could know nothing about the great news, if what Sarah said was true; the utmost he could do was to sense it in the air. But his look of subtle contentment was a sufficient annoyance in itself. It was the last straw, indeed, which broke the back of Eliza's self-control. When she turned again her words and her breath came with the leap of a mountain stream.

'I wonder you're not afraid, Sarah Thornthet, to be setting there reeling off lies like hanks o' cotton off a bobbin! Happen you're just thinking you'll get a rise out o' me and mine, but if that's the best you can do by way of a joke, well, I think nowt on't, and so I tell you! *Geordie* coming home wi' brass! *Geordie* wanting the Hall and such-like! Nay, Sarah, I might ha' believed the rest wi' a bit o' pulling and pushing, but yon last's taking it over far. Why, I'd as lief believe he was going to get the King's crown right out, wi' happen Witham Town Hall for a spot to live in! As for thinking o' me and my feelings and such-like stuff, you've never troubled that much about 'em to start bothering, now. There's only two ways about it, Sarah, and I reckon I know which it is. It's either a smart lie you've been telling, from end to end, or else it's never Geordie that's coming, but our Jim!'

She choked when she came to the last words, both from sudden nervousness and lack of breath, and again Sarah gave her well-bred laugh.

'I wouldn't be as hard o' faith as you, Eliza,' she said placidly—'not for a deal! It's you, not me, would have heard if Jim was coming home. What's Jim to do wi' me?'

'He'd a deal to do wi' you when he was in England, as everybody knows! Nay, you hated the sight o' him—that's true enough—but you were right keen on trying to set him agen me, all the same. What, the last letter I had from him—and terble saucy an' all—was blacking me over

summat I'd said of you as his lordship didn't like!
Nay, if he come home, Sarah, he'd come to you,
not me, and right glad you'd be to have him
while he'd a penny between his teeth! Ay, and
why shouldn't our lad ha' done as well as yours,
and happen better, come to that? He was the
smarter lad o' the two, and come o' smarter folk
—ay, but he *did* now, Sarah, so you'll kindly shut
your mouth! You've only to look at the way
we've done at Blindbeck, me and Will, and then
at the mess o' things you've made at yon pig-hull
on the marsh! It stands to reason our lad would
be the likely one to make out, just as it isn't in
reason to expect owt from yours!'

She came a step nearer as she finished, twisting
her plump hands, her voice, as it mounted higher,
full of bewilderment and angry tears.

'Will you swear to it Jim isn't coming, Sarah?'
she demanded—'will you swear? Will you swear
as it is your lad that's coming, and not mine?'

Sarah said, 'Ay, I will that!' in a hearty tone,
and with such absolute readiness that Eliza bit
her lip. 'If you've a Bible anywhere handy,' she
went on tranquilly, 'I'll swear to it right off.'

But already Eliza had drawn back in order to
follow a fresh trail. Quite suddenly she had
perceived the only means of getting at the truth.

'Nay, I'll not trouble you,' she sneered. ''Tisn't
worth it, after all. I shouldn't like our grand
Family Bible to turn yeller wi' false swearing!
Geordie's letter'll be proof enough, Sarah, now I
come to think on. I'll believe owt about Halls
and such-like, if you'll show me that!'

She came a step nearer still, holding out her
hand, and instantly Sarah's lips tightened and

her eyes narrowed. She might have had a dozen sacred letters about her, from the look of her, at that moment. It might have been Geordie's face itself that she guarded from the touch of Eliza's hands.

'Ay, I'd be like to show you his letter, wouldn't I?' she answered, with a wicked smile. 'You and me have been such terble friends all these years— I'd be like to show you owt from my bonny lad! Nay, Eliza, you know I'd shove it in t'fire unread, afore I'd let you as much as clap eyes on a single word!'

Eliza wheeled away from her with an angry oath, and began to walk to and fro, setting the loose planks jumping and creaking under her feet, and the china rattling and clinking on the shelves. Her hands worked in and out of each other with convulsive movements, and now and then she flung out her heavy arms. She was working herself into one of those storms which the folk at the farm knew only too well; but Sarah, who was the cause of it, did not seem to care. She, too, however, was breathing faster than before, and a faint colour had stayed in her waxen cheek. She still felt as if, in that last bout, she had protected something vital from Eliza's hands.

'I'll be bound it's Jim!' Eliza was saying senselessly, over and over again. 'I'll swear it's Jim!' . . . It was like a giant's voice, Sarah thought to herself, the voice of a cruel, clumsy giant-child. 'You're telling a lie, Sarah—a nasty lie! You're jealous, that's what it is—jealous and mean! *Geordie* wi' brass? Not likely! . . . Nay, it's Jim!'

'It's plain enough it's the brass you're after, and nowt else,' Sarah said in her cool tones. 'You'd have no use for the poor lad if he come back without a cent!'

But even while the words were on her lips, Eliza, creaking to and fro, was brought to a sudden halt. The thing that held her was a photograph of Jim, catching her eye in its frame of crimson plush. If he had been older when it was taken, it would have been banished long ago, but here he was only a mischievous baby, struggling in his mother's arms. Eliza stared at it as she stood in front of the mantelpiece, and quite suddenly she began to cry. The tears poured down her face, and her hands trembled and her body shook. Into the brutal voice came a note at which Sarah, unable to trace the cause, yet quivered in every nerve.

'Nay, then, Sarah, you're wrong, Sarah; you're dead wrong! I'd be glad to see him just for himself, I would that! He's been nowt but a trouble and disappointment all his life, but I'd be glad to see him, all the same.' She put out the plump fingers which Sarah loathed, and drew them caressingly over the baby face. 'I can't do wi' failures,' she added brokenly; 'they make me wild; and Jim was the only failure Blindbeck ever hatched. But for all that he was the bonniest baby of the lot, and there's times I never remember nowt but that. There's days I just ache for the sound of his voice, and fair break my heart to think he'll never come back.'

There was no doubting the sincerity of her grief, and the big sobs shaking their way through her shook Sarah, too. Her own lips trembled, and her eyes filled; her hands quivered on the arms of the chair. She could not see the pitiful fingers stroking the child's face, but she who had offered that worship herself needed little help to guess. She had her revenge in full as she sat and listened to the passion that never dies, forcing its way upward even through Eliza's leathern soul; but the revenge was a two-edged sword that wounded herself as well. All the generosity in her that was still alive and kind would have sprung to the surface instantly if the story had been true. She would have groped her way to Eliza's side in an effort to console, and perhaps the lifelong enemies might have drawn together for once. But the story was not true, and she had nothing to offer and no right of any sort to speak. She could only sit where she was and suffer and shake, hating herself more in this moment of absolute conquest than she had ever hated Eliza in her darkest hour.

But, as a matter of fact, Eliza's grief would have passed before she could even have tottered to her feet. Her own lips were still shaking when Eliza's had hardened again; her own eyes were still wet when Eliza's were dry with hate. The passion which for a brief moment had been self-less and sincere was turned once again into the channel of jealous rage. She swung round so swiftly that her sleeve caught the little frame, and it fell forward unnoticed with a sharp tinkle of broken glass.

'There's summat wrong about it all,' she cried venomously, 'and I'll not rest till I find out what it is! What's Geordie mean by landing up so smart, and leaving our Jim a thousand mile behind? It's a nasty sort o' trick, if it's nothing worse, seeing how they were thick as thieves as lads. I'll tell you what it is, Sarah, and you may swallow it as you can—if Geordie's gitten brass, it's because he's robbed it off our Jim! Like enough he's put an end to him for it, the poor, honest lad—knifed him . . . finished him . . . put him out o' the road . . . !'

The fierce malice of the voice penetrated into the passage, and carried its message into the kitchen and the yard. Will and Simon heard it at the stable door, and looked at each other and turned instantly towards the house. Passing the parlour window, they saw the women rigid on their feet, and felt the current of hate sweep strongly across their path. They had a glimpse of Sarah's face, white, blind and quiet: and Eliza's, vindictive, purple, and bathed with furious tears. Her heavy tone beat at the other's immobility as if with actual blows, and the glass in the cabinet rang and rang in sweet reply. Will quickened his pace as he neared the house, for he knew that Eliza did not always stop at words. Indeed, her hands were reaching out towards Sarah's throat at the very moment he stepped inside.

'Whisht, can't ye, Eliza!' he ordered roughly, his voice harsh with the swift reaction from the little space of content through which he and his brother had just passed. 'What's taken you, missis, to be going on like yon?'

He was now in the parlour, with Simon at his heels, while the company from the kitchen clustered round the door. Peering into the tiny arena round each other's heads, they giggled and whispered, curious and alarmed. Sarah could hear them stirring and gurgling just beyond her sight, and felt their rapacious glances fastened upon her face. Sally tried to push her way through to her aunt's side, but was stopped by the solid figure of Elliman, set in the very front. The lads had forsaken the milking to run to the window and peep in, and a dog lifted its bright head and planted its forefeet on the sill. All the life of the place seemed drawn to this little room, where at last the women were fighting things out to the very death.

'What's amiss, d'ye say?' Eliza echoed his speech. 'Nay, what *isn't* amiss! Here's Sarah has it her Geordie's a-coming home, but never a word as I can hear about our Jim!'

The eyes of the brothers met in a startled glance, and the red came painfully into Simon's face. Before they could speak, however, Eliza swept their intention from them like a western gale.

'What's come to Jim, I want to know? Why isn't it our Jim? Geordie's made his pile, so Sarah says, but I can't hear of a pile for Jim. He's dead, that's what it is! . . . Geordie's finished him, I'll swear! He's robbed him! . . . knifed him! . . . given him a shove in t'beck . . .!'

Again she made that threatening movement towards Sarah's throat, but Will put out his hand and caught her by the wrist. Both the giggles and whispers had died a sudden death, and the lads at the window pressed nearer and looked scared. Sally succeeded at last in forcing her way through, careless that Elliman suffered severely as she passed.

'For goodness' sake, stop it, mother!' she cried

sharply. 'You're fair daft! Can't you wait to
make a stir till Geordie's landed back? He'll tell
us right enough then what's happened to our
Jim.'

'He'll tell us nowt—nowt——!' Eliza began
again on a high note, but Simon threw up his
hand with a sudden snarl.

'Whisht, can't ye! You fair deafen a body,
Eliza!' he flung out. 'What's all this stir about
Geordie coming back?'

'It's a lie, that's what it is!' Eliza exploded
again and again he silenced her with an angry
'Whisht!' He kept his eyes on her a moment
longer, as if daring her to speak, and then let
them travel slowly and almost reluctantly to his
wife's face. He opened his lips to address her and
then changed his mind, turning instead to the
crew beyond the door.

'Tell me about it, can't you?' he demanded
angrily. 'One o' you speak up! Emily Marion—
Addison—you wi' the fat face!' He jerked a con-
temptuous thumb at Elliman, who went crimson
with extreme disgust. 'One o' you tell me the
meaning o' this precious hullaballoo!'

Elliman looked across to Sally for help, but did
not get it. Instead, she turned her eyes away,
ignoring his appeal.

'It's hardly my place to enlighten you, sir,' he
said, with an offended shrug, 'but I don't mind
telling you the little I know. Apparently your
son Geordie is expected soon, and with a full
purse in his pocket to buy him a welcome
home.'

'Geordie's coming back, d'ye say?' Simon
stared at him with bewildered eyes.

'So Mrs. Thornthwaite has given us to understand.'

'And wi' brass? Plenty o' brass? *Geordie* wi' brass?'

'Enough and to spare, if all we're told is true.'

'Ay, but that's just what it isn't!' Eliza broke out on a peacock scream, and this time Will actually shook her into silence. The poignancy of the moment had hushed the rest of the audience into complete quiet. There was no sound in the room but Eliza's breathing as Simon turned again to look at his wife.

'What's it all about, Sarah?' he asked quietly, though his voice shook. 'You never said nowt about Geordie coming, to me.'

In the pause that followed, Sally drew away from her aunt's side, as if conscious that this moment was for the two of them alone. The silence waited for Sarah's answer, but she could not bring herself to speak. In the heat of her victory she had forgotten that Simon also would hear the lying tale. It was the only hitch in the splendid machinery of the lie, but it was enough in itself to bring the whole of it to the ground. Here was Simon in front of her, asking for the truth, and if a hundred Elizas had been present she could still have given him nothing but the truth. But indeed, at that moment, Eliza, and all that Eliza stood for, was swept away. In that hush and sudden confronting of souls Sarah and Simon were indeed alone.

'Geordie's never coming, is he, Sarah?' he asked anxiously. 'Nay, you've dreamed it, my lass! And he's rich, d'ye say?—why, that settles it, right out! Why, it was nobbut the other day he was writing home for brass!'

Still she did not speak, and quite suddenly he was wroth, vexed by her mask-like face and the sudden diminishing of his hope.

'Losh, woman!' he cried angrily. 'You look half daft! Is yon lad of ours coming, or is he not? Is it truth you're telling me, or a pack o' lies?'

She stirred then, moved by the cheated sound in his angry voice. She gave a sigh. The fooling of Eliza had been utterly great and glorious, but it had come to an end. 'It was just lies,' she heard herself saying in a passionless tone, and then with a last twinge of regret, she sighed again.

Eliza's scream of 'I knew it! I knew it!' merged in the chorus of exclamation from the group about the door. Will said nothing, fixing his sister-in-law with his kindly gaze, but Simon fell back muttering, and staring as if afraid. He wondered, looking at her unemotional face, whether the trouble about her eyes was beginning to touch her brain. She herself had said there was no knowing what blind weather might possibly do, no telling what a blind body's brain might someday suddenly breed. . . .

He came back to the consciousness of Eliza's voice as a man from the dead hears the roar of life as he returns.

'I wonder you're not struck down where you stand, Sarah Thornthet! I wonder you're not liggin' dead on t'floor! But you'll be punished for it, right enough; you'll be paid for it, never fear! *You*'ll see, summat'll happen to you afore so long—I shouldn't wonder if it happened before morn! Like enough, the next news as we have o'

Geordie'll be as he's dead or drowned. . . . I'll serve you a slap on t'lugs, Will, if you can't shape to let me be!'

It was Sally who saved the situation for the second time, that day.

'Fetch the trap, Uncle Simon, and look sharp about it!' she commanded smartly, 'and you come and set down, Aunt Sarah, until it's round. Let her be, can't you!' she added roughly, flinging round on her mother. 'She's that tired and put out she don't know what she's at.'

She shook her fist at the window, and the faces disappeared like morning frost. Then she turned on the others and ordered them out, too.

'You'd best be getting about your business!' she commanded them, hand on hip. 'You should be in t'dairy this minute, Mary Phyllis—you know that as well as me. I'd think shame o' myself, Mr. and Mrs. Addison, to be helping other folks wi' their weekly wash! Same to you, Elliman Wilkinson, and a bit over, come to that! You're not one o' the family yet by a long chalk, my lad; nay, nor like to be, neither, if you don't see to mend your ways!'

Eliza still lingered, however, loath that anything should be left unsaid, but Sally ushered her resolutely to the door. She protested to the last inch, and the hand that had been denied judgment on Sarah flew up and slapped Sally's face. The girl looked at her with scornful eyes.

'Ay, you can't keep your hands off folk, can you?' she said bitterly. 'You never could. I remember Jim saying he fair hated you for it when we were barns. That was why he always liked Aunt Sarah a deal better than he liked you!'

'You'll find other folk free wi' their hands,'
Eliza stormed, 'if you're that free wi' your im-
pident tongue! Yon fool of an Elliman'll stand
no nonsense, for all he looks so new-milk soft!
Not that he wants any truck wi' you at all, as far
as I can see. It's Mary Phyllis he can't take his
eyes off, and no wonder, neither. She was always
a sight better-looking than you, and she's younger,
by a deal. You're that old and teptious you fair
turn the cream sour just by being along wi't in
t'house! Nay, I reckon you can put wedding and
such-like out o' your head as soon as you like!
You'll never have a house of your own, or a man
to put in it; and as for barns o' your own to slap,
why, you'll never have none o' *them* . . .!'

She said the rest to the closed door, a stout,
oaken door which even she was reluctant to
attack. In the few pauses that she allowed herself
she could hear nothing inside the room, and
presently, tiring of the one-sided contest, she
waddled heavily away along the passage. She
was in the dairy, a minute later, and saw through
the window the brothers yoking the old horse.
Through the window, too, she caught scraps
of their talk, and strained her ears eagerly to
catch its bent. As if by magic the anger left her
face, and a little smile grew happily on her lips.
She even hummed a little tune to herself, as
she watched and listened, leaning against the
frame. . . .

The silence persisted in the room that she had
left, as if the air was so laden with words that it
would hold no more. Sarah groped her way to
the rocking-chair and sat down again to wait.
Sally went to the window, and stared miserably

into the yard. So they waited together until they heard the rattle of the wheels along the stones. . . .

VII

Even now, however, the Blindbeck comedy was not quite played out. Eliza had still to give it its finishing touch. The lately-routed audience must have been conscious of this, for they assembled again in order to watch the Thornthwaites take their leave. As a rule, the Simons simply faded away, unperceived and unsped of anybody but Will. They were not welcome when they came, and they were not lamented when they went away. But to-day Sarah had managed to touch the imagination of the crowd, arousing unwilling admiration and even respect. The Addisons, for instance, though outwardly badly shocked, rejoiced by proxy in a crime which they would never have had the courage to commit themselves. Even Elliman was heard to remark that Sarah's psychology seemed possibly worthy of study, after all. The main motive with all, however, was a sneaking hope that, on some ground or another, the opponents might go for each other again.

As if by accident, therefore, they drifted out of the house, and on Sarah's appearance were to be found sitting on rails or pig-sty walls, or leaning in graceful attitudes against the porch. Sarah could not see them, but Simon could, and divided a scowl of dislike amongst the lot. The Thornthwaites were actually settled in the trap when Eliza came bustling after them into the yard.

It was such a different Eliza, however, that at first it looked as if the audience were to be cheated of their scene. The virulent harridan of ten minutes ago had vanished as if she had never been. This Eliza was hearty, smiling, serene, the smooth-faced, smooth-tongued mocker whom Sarah detested most. Even her hair and dress, lately dishevelled by rage, were now as tidy and sleek as the fur of a well-brushed cat. She came to a halt close beside the wheel, and Sarah started when she heard her speak.

'So you're off, are you, Sarah? Ay, well, you'll be best at home! I reckon our Sally's right, and you're not yourself at all. Mind and see doctor again, first thing as ever you can. It's a bad sign, they say, to go making up fancy tales. Folks as get telling lies is framing for softening of the brain.'

Will looked back with a frown as he hurried on to open the gate.

'We've had enough o' that, missis!' he called sharply. 'Just you let Sarah be!'

Mrs. Will tossed her head, but managed to preserve her compassionate air.

'Losh, master!' she reproached him loudly. 'You've no call to speak so sharp. I'm meaning kindly enough by poor Sarah here, I'm sure! She's welcome to tell lies till they turn her black in the face, but it isn't healthy for her, all the same. I shouldn't like to see poor Sarah in Garland's Asylum, or some such spot as yon. Ay, well, we'll be having her close at hand afore so long, and then we can do our best for her ourselves!'

Sarah started a second time when she said that, and the pig-sty audience brightened and pricked its ears. Simon muttered an oath and pulled at

the horse until it sidled and backed, forcing the
subtle tormentor to retreat.

'You stand back, missis,' he cried angrily,
waving a threatening whip, 'and take your long
tongue with you, or it'll be tripping us in
t'road!'

There was a burst of laughter at this show of
wit, and Eliza flared instantly into open war.
She raised her voice after the departing pair,
stepping back heavily upon Elliman's feet.

'You'll have to speak different from that, Mr.
Thornthet,' she called shrilly, 'if you're coming
to Blindbeck to act as our hired man!'

The laughter broke out again, and then stopped,
cut short. Simon, red to the ears, raised the
whip violently above the horse's back, but it was
checked before it descended by Sarah's out-
stretched hand.

'Bide a minute, Simon,' she said quietly. 'Just
hold on. What's Eliza meaning to say by that?'

Simon looked helplessly about him, noting the
interested gaping faces on all sides. 'Ax me on
t'road,' he said desperately, yearning to get away.
'It's time we were getting on, missis. Ax me on
t'road!'

'Nay, ax him now, and ha' done wi' it, Sarah!'
Eliza jeered, advancing again. 'Or ax me, if you
want, and I'll tell you mighty sharp! Likely
you've been wondering what's to come o' you
when you leave the farm? Ay, well, our cowman's job is going begging, at present, and I hear
your master's thinking o' taking it on.'

There was a pause, after that, in which even
the pig-sty audience was hushed as mice, and the
fretting horse itself was suddenly still. Those

nearest to Sarah heard her give a sigh, the same little sigh with which she had loosed her hold on the parlour dream. The next moment Simon had thankfully eased the reins, and the trap went creaking and jolting out of the still yard. . . .

Eliza watched it triumphantly until the very last, and then, bursting into a laugh, turned expectantly for applause. But for once her usually appreciative audience failed her of her due. They avoided her eyes and looked at their boots, or leaned over the pig-sty walls and pretended a passionate interest in the pigs. The Addisons, in whom Christian charity was apt to rise and fall like a turned-on jet, murmured tepid thanks for their entertainment, and hurried away. Even the smug cousin refused to play up to Eliza for once, partly because of a latent fineness of feeling which she had hurt, but chiefly because she had trodden on his toes. Turning his back determinedly upon Mary Phyllis, he bent to whisper something in Sally's ear. She hesitated a moment, lifting her eyes to his sobered face, and then followed him slowly towards the track across the fields.

VIII

OUTSIDE the farmyard wall, Sarah again put out a hand to Simon's arm. 'Yon's Taylor's spot, isn't it?' she enquired, as the cottage came up. 'Just hold up a minute, and let me see.'

He obeyed, watching her nervously as she bent and peered at the house, and wondering uneasily what she was about. She knew the house well enough, both inside and out, so she could not be stopping to look at it just for that. She must be trying to form some impression of it that was wholly new, perhaps picturing it as it would be when she had come to live in it herself.

When he found that she did not speak, he began to offer clipped remarks, anxiously pointing out objects that she was quite unable to see.

'It's a good house, missis. . . . You'll remember it's a tidy spot. There's a fairish garden for cabbishes and the like, and a bit of a drying-ground as well. As for berry-bushes, there's gooseberry and black currant and red . . . and danged if there isn't a few rasps over at far side wall an' all!'

Sarah looked away from the house the moment he started to speak, as if some spell were broken by the sound of his voice. 'Ay,' she said, with a total lack of interest, and staring ahead. . . . 'Now, master, we'd best get on.'

Simon, cut off in mid-flight, repeated 'Rasps!' in a feeble tone, and again Sarah said 'Ay,' and requested him to get on. He drove away rather reluctantly, looking behind him as he went, and muttering of Taylor's rasps and cabbishes until they were finally lost to sight.

Now once more they were in the high-flanked lane, with Blindbeck and all that Blindbeck stood for fallen away at last. The cross went with them, indeed, but the calvary dropped behind. The horse, turned homeward, and, encouraged by Will's corn, showed a sudden freakish revival of vanished youth. Bicycles met and passed them in the narrow road, sliding by like thistledown on a wind, while the riders saw only an elderly couple apparently half asleep. Yet even the dullest farm-lad would have cried aloud to them if he had known to what they went. He would

have flung himself off his bicycle and barred the
road, a humble but valiant imitation of an angel
of God.

Evening was coming, but the day was still alive,
incredibly long as the afternoon had seemed.
Simon's old watch, put right that morning in
Witham, asserted that it was only half-past four.
The atmosphere had never been really light, and
only imperceptibly was it drawing down to dusk.
The grey seemed to have deepened and settled
a little, but that was all. It was a day on which
people forgot the time, as Mr. Dent had said; a
day when they had every excuse for forgetting
the right time. Simon felt suddenly as though
he had never seen the sun either rise or set for at
least a week. Yesterday there had been only a
swift setting, hurriedly blotted out, and to-day,
if there had been any fugitive brightness of fare-
well, it must have passed while they were still at
the farm. The night was coming unduly to the
grey-green land which had never had its meed
of sun, just as the night came unfairly to lives
whose share of glamour and glory had been
missed. He longed to see a light spring out of the
west, showing the silver water in a shining line,
and re-tinting the heavy, neutral-coloured earth.

Sun—evening sun lying over the sea—would
have made things easier for both of them, but
especially for his wife. Even though there was
so little that she could see, the warmth and
light would at least have lain tenderly upon her
lids. Trouble and change were always easier to
bear under a smiling sky; it did not mock at the
trouble, as smiling faces so often seemed to do.
Rain and the dark seemed to narrow a trouble

in, so that change was a nameless peril into which
each step was into a void. But there was to be no
sun for these lost folk who seemed to be straying
all the day long; only the unstirred breath of the
mist in the blotted west, filling the mighty bowl
at whose bottom lay the sea.

They felt strange with each other, now that
they were alone, because of all that the other had
done while the two of them were apart. Simon's
sudden decision was as inexplicable to his wife as
her afternoon's jest with Eliza had seemed to
him. In his place she would never have stooped
to make of herself the younger brother's man;
she would have worked for the hardest driver
amongst them sooner than that. Even the close
affection between the brothers could not dignify
the position in her eyes. She could understand
something of Simon's yearning towards the farm,
but Sarah was never the sort of which they make
door-keepers in Heaven. She would never really
have understood the strength of the pull, even
with no Eliza set like a many-eyed monster on
the farmyard wall. He, on the other hand, could
not even pretend to grasp the lying jest, but then
the vision of the parlour had been granted to her
and not to him.

Both their minds, however, were at work more
on the change that was coming than on Sarah's
sudden craze, since always the pressing business
of life must supersede the dream. Simon, indeed,
did not want to think about Sarah's behaviour
further than he could help, because of that sinister
saying about the doings of blind brains. As for
Sarah herself, she had done with the dream for
ever in that moment when she came face to

face with the limits of her lie. It had had its
tremendous hour in the down-treading of a lifelong foe, but in that one stupendous achievement
it had finally passed. Never again would she be
able to shut herself in the spell, until the blind
saw and the lost spoke, and the sea was crossed
in a leap. Never again would she be able to
believe that Geordie might come home.

In spite of their shameful departure, fast fading,
however, from his mind, Simon was already
planning the bitter-sweet prospect of their near
return. Like so many ideas impossible and even
repellent at the start, this had already become
natural and full of an acid charm. For the time
being he was content to ignore the drawbacks of
the position, and to concentrate only upon its
obvious gains. His mind, hurrying forward over
the next few months, was already disposing of
stock, farm-implements, and surplus household
gear; and in his complete absorption he forgot
that he was not alone, and kept jerking out frag-
ments of disjointed speech. Sarah allowed him
to amuse himself after this fashion for some time,
and then broke dryly into his current of thought.

'You may as well tell me what's settled, and
get it by with,' she observed in a sardonic tone.
'So far, even Eliza seems to know more about it
than me. You and Will seem to ha' fixed things
up wi' a vengeance, that you have! You'd best
to tell me how it come about, instead of booing
away to yourself like a badly calf.'

'Nay, it was all fixed that sharp,' Simon
grumbled, with an injured air, though highly
relieved at heart to hear her speak. 'There was
no time to ax nobody nor nowt. I'm still a bit

maiselt about it, myself, for the matter o' that. I don't know as I'll be that surprised if I hear to-morrow it's all off. As for Eliza, it fair beats me how she could ha' got wind of it so smart! She likely hid herself somewheres when we was talking it out; though she's not that easy to miss —gert spying toad!'

He brisked considerably, now that the first awkwardness was past, and went on to tell her, after his usual backwards and forwards fashion, exactly how the new arrangement had come about.

'It's not much to crack on, I dare say,' he finished, pleading with her across the disapproving silence which had again risen between them like a wall, 'but, when all's said and done, it's a sight better than I'd looked for, by a deal. I'd ha' been bound to hire myself somewheres, to help us make out, and there isn't a decenter master in t'countryside than Will. It's a deal better than being odd-job man at some one-horse spot, or maybe scrattin' up weeds and such-like at some private house. There'll be a decent wage, think on, and milk—ay, and happen a load o' coal an' all. Will'll see as we're rightly done by, never fret! We'll be right comfortable, I'm sure. Will says his lasses'll give you a hand wi' washing and the like, and if happen we get a good sale, we might run to a bit o' help ourselves. You'll miss t'horse and cart, I reckon, but we'll find a way out o' yon, as well. If you felt as you fancied a bit of a ride, Will'd like enough loan me a horse and trap.'

He was coaxing her for all he was worth, but neither the coaxing nor the explanation seemed

to get any farther than her ears. Again he felt
the spasm of irritation which he had felt in the
parlour, and was at the same time reminded of
its original cause.

'I don't say it'll be over pleasant for either on
us,' he went on vexedly, as she did not open her
lips, 'but you'll likely admit I did the best I could
for us, all the same. It's a sad pity you and Eliza
pull together so bad, but it's over late to think o'
mending it now. Anyway, you did nowt to mend
it by telling yon string o' lies, this afternoon!
What, in the name o' goodness, made you act so
strange?'

She moved, then, a touch of the afternoon
glamour reaching from Blindbeck and following
her down the lane.

'Nay, I don't know. . . . Things come over
folk, now and then. I'm right sorry, though, if I
set you thinking it was the lad.'

'I've given up thinking owt o' the sort long
since,' he said dejectedly. 'I should ha' thought
you would ha' done the same an' all.'

'Things come over folk,' she repeated, unwilling to say more, and he nodded his head, relieved
by her softer tone.

'You'll try to make up your mind to Blindbeck,
will you, missis?' he pressed on nervously, hoping
her mood would last. 'It's a bad best, maybe,
but I nobbut did what I could.'

She gave a sharp sigh, but her voice was firm.
'Ay, I'll make up my mind to it, after a bit.'

'It's a big change at our time of life, but you'll
settle, never fear.'

'Ay, I'll settle all right. Don't you fret.'

'It's a good shop, Sarah.'

'Ay.'

'And Will's a right good sort.'

'Oh, ay.'

The sudden gentleness of her mood prompted him to a further unburdening of his soul. He leaned forward a little in the trap, staring over the grey fields, and with the note of pleading rising and falling in his tone.

'I don't mind telling you now, Sarah, but I've been fair fretted out o' my senses all this while. There's been times I've felt like just making off on t'sands, and letting tide settle it for me for good an' all. Ay, and by gox! it very near come about, too, one day when I was mooning along and not looking where I was at! But there was you to see to, and I couldn't rightly bring myself to chuck up the sponge. 'Tisn't as if the lad was dead, neither—there was that as well. He's as good as dead, likely, but it's a different thing, all the same. Folks can get along on a mighty little hope—same as yon old horse as died just when it was learning to live on nowt! We've come to a bonny pass, these days, you and Geordie an' me, but the world isn't past bearing as long as the three on us is over sod.'

It was with a sense of enlightenment and escape that they came out finally on to the high road, for in the cleft of the lane every curve of the land stole what little clarity was left to the slowly withdrawing earth. Even Sarah was faintly conscious of lightened lids, as well as of easier breathing as the borders of the road drew farther apart. In the lane they had been high, looming presences, over-close to the lurching wheels, but now they ceased to oppress her, though she was still aware

that they marched with her as she went. It was
as if the furniture of the land were being withdrawn into the wings before the curtain of night
was really down; yet even in its slow departure
it still formed the picture and dominated the
scene. The only real comfort for brain and eyes
was on the unfurnished marsh, where even the
fenced roads lifted themselves as often as not
above their fences to look abroad.

There was more life, also, on the open road—
cycles and traps, and people walking in twos and
threes; motor-cars, too, at which Simon never so
much as glanced aside, though now they were
really beginning to look like ghosts in the sinking
light. Even when there was nobody on the road
there was still the sense of being part of an unseen
train, the link which binds traveller to traveller
on every principal highway in the land, but
especially on those which run north and south.
The link strengthens and the thrill deepens as
the day lengthens and the hours go on. Each
wonders instinctively to what home the other is
hastening before he is overtaken by the dark.
From each to each at the hour of dusk passes
the unconscious God-speed, uniting all who are
drawing together towards the adventure of the
night.

And, for Simon and Sarah, as for all, either
man or beast, even in this bitter hour, there was
the comfort of the road that goes home. There is
always a lamp set high in the house to which one
returns, even though it be poor and empty and
dark. The greatest sorrow awaiting one at the
end is not really a sorrow until one steps inside.
The ease of the road home is the ineffable ease of

the mind. Stout hearts and limbs may carry us out, and barely suffice to stagger us back, but the running and leaping mind can comfort the body on. There is always a lamp set high at the end of the road that is going home. . . .

Not until they had lost it would they realise the perpetual consolation of that long-accustomed road. Times without number they had travelled it, seething with anger and hate, and yet always they were the richer for having passed that way. Simon, busily thinking of Blindbeck and all the advantages of the wealthy farm, did not know that he was putting his real wealth from him with every thought. Yet he would know it all the rest of his life when he drove a road that was not consecrated by the years; when the folk that hailed them in passing were not part of a lifelong chain; when the turns of the road were no longer pictures and books, with each house where it should be and would be for all time; when he stopped at a gate in the dusk and knew it was not his; when he entered a meaningless building at last and knew it was not home. . . .

But just for the moment he was thinking neither of the immediate present nor of the greater part of his long-reaching past. His mind, unusually stimulated by the day's events, swung easily to and fro between the future at Blindbeck and the far-off boyhood which he had spent with Will. Blindbeck had never been his home in any sense, but his call to Blindbeck was nevertheless the call of the past. They would renew their youth for each other, the two old men, and forget when they were together that they were old. They turned instinctively to each other, as all turn

to those who can recreate for them the young
beginnings of their lives. On the marsh Simon
always felt immeasurably old, weighted as with
an actual burden by the years. He saw himself looking behind him at them as at monsters
created in his pride, which now and for ever were
out of his control. With Will beside him, they
would lie in front as they used to do, rolling
pasture-lands still untouched by the plough of
time. Because they had been young together, it
would be impossible for them to be really old.
Because they had been young together, they
could look, smiling, shoulder to shoulder, into the
unbelievable grave.

Not that his longing had any such definite
frame of thought as this, though he was aware
that in it had lain the motive which had fixed his
mind. He only moved toward its fulfilment as all
untutored souls move naturally towards release
from strain. He scarcely remembered Sarah
after their talk had come to an end that was
hardly an end, like an unravelled cord of which
no one troubles to count the untwisted strands.
That mighty leap which he was taking across the
years carried him well above both Sarah's and
Geordie's heads. The school-years, the climbing,
running, hungry years were more distinct to him
than the heavy, responsible years of marriage
and middle life. He saw himself and Will running after the hounds, paddling in calm lakes of
gold-shot evening tides, skating by slowly-rising
moons. He saw a raw lad going shyly but stolidly
to his first place, already a man in the awed
estimation of the brother left behind. He heard
the clink of the first money he had ever earned,

which had gone straight from his pocket into the
family purse. He had handed it over without a
twinge of regret, and his empty hands had continued to thrill with pride. Later, he had begged
a couple of shillings for himself and Will, and had
never thought of the money then or since but as
a gift. . . .

They came at last to the dangerous, right-
angled turn which dropped them down to the
marsh, and, as the horse began to jerk itself
down the hill, a car passed slowly above them
along the open road. Although the day still
lingered, the tail-light was already lit, as if the
car were setting out on a journey instead of going
home. Yet it went slowly and almost reluctantly,
like a man who looks over his shoulder all the
while. It was as if it was only waiting its opportunity to turn itself in its tracks. But all the time
it was drifting gradually away, and the red light,
that could hardly as yet impress itself on the dusk,
seemed to hesitate for a moment at a curve of the
road, and then, as if a hand had been clapped
in front of it, was suddenly gone.

The drop from the highway was like being
dropped from a cliff, so distinct was the change
to the loneliness of the marsh. The link was
broken which made them members of a purposed
line, leaving them mere strayed wanderers of
whom nobody was aware. The few farmhouses,
lifeless-looking in the deadened light, stared
always towards great distances over their puny
heads. The few trees sprang up before them,
suddenly strange, acquiring an almost violent
personality against the meaningless scene.

The straight miles dragged reluctantly past

their heavy wheels, and on the unending road they seemed to go forward without purpose and to be set on a journey that had no goal. When at length the stretches of meadow and cropped land gave place to the pale-coloured desert of the sand, there seemed no possible reason why one should cease and the other begin. Away out behind the mist there was a living, moving tide, but here on the marsh there was no consciousness of tide. Things just stopped, that was all, and from the garden became the waste, just as the growth and renewal of life had stopped for the old pair, leaving nothing but desolation before their feet.

Yet still the earth was with them, and Simon turned his eyes again and again to its vague outlines with relief. Across the bay the cone of the Knott still held to its tangibility and form, protesting against the swamping hand of night. The crown of it, fitted with wood as closely as with a cap, was darker against the sky than the shadowy slopes on which the houses climbed. And, nearer inland still, on the low edge of shore that was like a trail of smoke on the farther side of the sands, a blur of formless yet purposeful grey showed where the tiny hamlet of Sandyeat clustered about the 'Ship.'

Sandholes was in sight now, and the horse quickened its pace, triumphing over the last few wearisome yards. As they approached the house, with its white face set on a body of looming buildings behind, they had as always a mingled sensation of sadness and relief. Not that the place was sad to them because of its dreary emptiness set amongst formless fields. In the course of years it had become for them merely an atmosphere, not a thing of sight. They were only depressed by it because for them it was the heart of failure and loss. And in the same way they were relieved by it, dignified, sanctuaried and consoled, because this was their hiding-place against the world, and here the heart of their few memories of joy.

The house was dark, but they were accustomed to that; used to the door that would not open, however they knocked, and the windows that for ever would never frame a face, however they hailed. They were used to that stumbling into the place in the folding dark, to the striking of a match that brought them nothing but the dreary waiting rigidity of the things they had left behind. They were used, too, to an uprising fear on the struck light that some terrible change might have taken place in the empty house; that even the waiting things might have played them false while they were gone. . . .

So lonely looked the place, that it seemed as if it might even revenge itself upon those who had the temerity to awaken it during that sinking hour; but, as they reached the gate, the old dog asleep in a loose box aroused himself to a hoarse, recognising bark. The few cows, also, waiting to be fed, sent out low murmurings at the sound of the coming wheels. And as they finally rattled into the uneven yard, a woman's figure stood up and waved to them from the sea-wall.

MAY

I

THE afternoon which had seen Sarah's short-lived splendour had been sweet also for May. Sweeter, indeed, since for her there was no clashing of fierce passions to jar the tender witchery of her mood. And though the glamour was of the past—a sheet of gold as of sunlight far at the back of her mind—a sea of gold from which she moved ever inward towards the darkness of the hills—a tongue of light had suddenly darted from it to stream like a golden, wind-blown ribbon over her path. That light was the knowledge that in her own hands lay the possibility of Geordie's return.

Youth came back to her with the thought, and she sat straighter still in the trap, holding her unused whip at a jaunty angle across the elastic bar of the reins. The good horse swung homewards in a generous stride; the bright wheels of the dog-cart flashed through the dull country like a whirled autumn leaf. The passers-by found a special sweetness in her ready smile, because it reflected the secret in her heart. As they went on their way they said what they always said—that it was a marvel she had not married, long ago.

Yet the secret, fair as it was, had also the folly of all great ventures; since, in laying her hands upon the future, she risked the memory that had coloured her whole life. To bring Geordie home might mean nothing but disappointment for herself, sordid disappointment and shame for a mis-spent girlish dream. Things would be different,

N   416 at the very best; part of the memory would have to go. But the chief people to be considered were the old folks who had so often been the footballs of fate. Nothing that she might fear on her own account should stand in the way of this sudden fulfilment for a frustrated old man, this light to the eyes for an old woman going blind. In any case May was the sort that would tenderly handle the cracked and mended pot right up to the moment of dissolution at the well. No disappointment that Geordie could bring her would remain sordid for very long. Out of her shattered idols her wisdom and humour would gather her fresh beauty; clear-eyed, uplifting affection for youthful worship, and pity and tenderness for passion.

It was true that Sarah had already rejected her offer—brutally, almost, in her determination that May should suffer no further for her son. But May had already almost forgotten the rough sentences which for the time being had slammed the opening door in her eager face. Sarah was strong, she knew, but she herself, because of love in the past and pity in the present, felt stronger still. She said to herself, smiling, that sooner or later she would find an argument that would serve. Sooner or later, Sarah would yield, and share with secret delight in the surprise that they would so gaily prepare for the old man. Sooner or later the boat would put out from port that carried the lost lad—Geordie, with his pockets empty but his heart full, and every nerve of him reaching towards his home.

Now she had turned the end of the bay, and was running along the flat road that hugged the curve of the shore. Below on her right were the sands, almost within flick of her whip, with the river-channel winding its dull length a hundred yards away. Beyond it, the sand narrowed into the arm of the marsh, until the eye caught the soft etching of the Thornthwaite farm, set on the faint gold and green of the jutting land.

The inn, low, white-faced, dark, with all the light of it in the eyes that looked so far abroad, was very quiet when she came to it about three o'clock. The odd-job man was waiting about to take her horse, and she paused to have a word or two with him in the yard. Then she went briskly into the silent place, and at once the whole drowsy air of it stirred and became alive. The spotlessness of the house seemed to take on a sparkling quality from the swift vitality of her presence. The very fire seemed to burn brighter when she entered, and the high lights on the steels and brasses to take a finer gleam. Her father called to her from the room where he lay upstairs, and her buoyant tread, as she went up, seemed to strengthen even his numb limbs and useless feet.

She sat by his bed for some time, telling him all the news, and conveying as much as she could of the hiring and marketing stir combined. This particular person had wished to know how he was; the other had sent him a message to be delivered word for word. One had a grandmother who had died in similar case; another a remedy that would recover him in a week. Bits of gossip she had for him, sketches of old friends; stories of old traits cropping up again which made him chuckle and cap them from the past. By the time she had finished he was firmly linked again to life, and had forgotten that deadly detachment which oppresses the long-sick. Indeed, he almost forgot, as he listened, that he had not been in Witham, himself, hearing the gossip with his own ears and seeing the familiar faces with his own eyes. For the time being he was again part of that central country life, the touchstone by which country-folk test reality and the truth of things, and by contact with which their own identity is intensified and preserved.

But her eyes were turned continually to the window as she chatted and laughed, dwelling upon the misty picture even when they were not followed by her mind. Only her brain answered without fail when her gaze travelled to the farm on the farther shore. Gradually the picture shadowed and dimmed in line, but still she sat by the bed and laughed with her lips while her heart looked always abroad. Neither she nor her father ever drew a blind in the little inn. They had lived so long with that wide prospect stretching into the house that they would have stifled mentally between eyeless walls.

She talked until he was tired, and then she made his tea, and left him happy with the papers which she had brought from Witham. Her own tea she ate mechanically, with the whole of her mind still fixed on the promise of the day, and when she had finished she was drawn to the window again before she knew. The Thorn-thwaites would be home by now, she concluded, looking out. Tired and discouraged, they would be back again at the farm, feeling none of the quivering hope which lifted and thrilled her heart. Sarah would not even dwell on the offer,

having put it by for good, and Simon did not as
much as know that there had been an offer at all.
They would creep to bed and sleep drearily, or
wake drearily against their will, while she would
wake of her own accord in order to clasp her
purpose and find it still alive. She could not bear
the thought of the long, blank night which would
so soon be wrapping them round; even a stubborn
refusal of her hope would be a better friend to
them than that. Stronger and stronger grew the
knowledge within her that she must see them
before they slept. It was for their sake, she told
herself, at first, thirsting to be across, and then,
as she clinched her decision, knew it was also for
her own.

She went upstairs again to put on her coat and
hat, wondering as she did so what her father
would have to say. He would be sure to enquire
what took her across the sands so late, yet he
would wonder and fret if she left him without a
word. Geordie's name had dropped into silence
between them for many a year, and, lately as she
had spoken it to Sarah, it would be hard to speak
it now. She knew only too well what her father
would think of her offer of hard-saved gold. He
had always been bitter against Geordie for her
sake, and would want no wastrel fetched overseas
to play on her pity again. She stole half-way
down the stairs, and then was vexed with herself
and went up again with a resolute tread. Once
more she hesitated, with her hand on the door-
latch, and then it slipped from her finger and she
found herself in the room.

Fleming looked up from his paper with his
faded eyes. 'Off again, lass?' he demanded,

noticing how she was dressed. 'Is there a pill-gill Milthrop way to-night?'

She shook her head.

'Not as I know of. . . . Nay, I'm sure there's not.' She stood staring at him, uncertain what to say, and then her eyes, as if of their own accord, turned back towards the sands. 'I just felt like going out a bit again, that's all.'

'Likely you're going up road for a crack wi' Mrs. Bridge?'

'Nay . . . I didn't think o' going there.'

'To t'station, happen?'

'Nor that, neither. . . .' There was a little pause. 'Just—out,' she added, and the note in her voice seemed to reach before her over the sandy waste. Fleming heard it, and saw the track of her gaze as well.

'What's up, lass?' he asked quietly, letting his paper drop. 'What d'you want to do?'

She braced herself, then, swinging round to him with one of her cheerful laughs. 'You'll think I'm daft, I know,' she said, looking down at him with dancing eyes, 'but I'm right set on seeing Mrs. Thornthet again to-night. We'd a deal to say to each other this morning, but we didn't finish our talk. I thought I could slip over sand and back before it was dark.'

Fleming looked perturbed.

'It's over late for that, isn't it?' he asked. 'Light's going pretty fast an' all. Hadn't you best bide till morning, and gang then?'

'I don't feel as I can. I'm set on going to-night. I've often been across as late, you'll think on. I'll take right good care.'

'What about tide?'

'Not for a couple of hours yet, and I've not that much to say. Boat's ready alongside channel; it nobbut wants shoving off. I'll be there and back before you can say knife.'

'Ay, well, then, you'd best be off, and look sharp about it!' Fleming conceded in a reluctant tone. 'I'll have t'lamp put in winder as usual to set you back. Don't you get clattin' now and forget to see if it's there.'

'I'll look out for it, don't you fret. Like as not I'll never go inside the house. There's just something I want to make sure of before I sleep.'

She nodded brightly and began to move away, but he called her back before she reached the door. With the quickness of those who lie long in a sick room, he had noticed the change in her atmosphere at once. Restlessness and impatience were strange things to find in May, and there was a touch of excitement in her manner as well. He looked at her thoughtfully as she retraced her steps.

'Is there any news o' that wastrel lad o' theirs? Happen he's thinking o' coming back?'

The words spoken from another's mouth brought a rush of certainty to her longing mind. She answered him confidently, as if she held the actual proof.

'That's it, father! That's right.' She laughed on a buoyant, happy note. 'Our Geordie's coming home!'

'To-night?' Fleming's mouth opened. 'D'ye mean he's coming *to-night*?'

'Nay, I don't know about that!' She laughed again. 'But it'll be before so long. I feel as sure about it as if he was knocking at Sandholes door!'

'You've no call to be glad of it, as I can see,' Fleming said, with a touch of fretfulness in his tone. 'Are you thinking o' wedding him after all this time?'

Her head drooped a little.

'I'm past thinking o' that, and he'll have been past it, long ago. I'm just glad for the old folks' sake, that's all. It's like as if it was somebody dead that was coming back, so that I needn't believe in death and such-like any more. It's like as if it's myself as is coming back—as if I should open door and see the lass I used to be, outside.'

'I'd be glad to see you settled afore I went, but not wi' an idle do-nowt as'd spoil your life. It'll be queer to me if Geordie Thornthet's made much out. He was a wastrel, right enough, for all his wheedlin' ways.'

'I'm past thinking o' marriage,' she said again. 'It's just what it means to the old folks, poor old souls!'

'Ay. They've had a mighty poor time, they have that.' He sighed, thinking of many a tale of woe unfolded by Simon beside his bed. Then he looked up at her with a whimsical smile. 'They'd nobbut the one barn, same as your mother and me, and there's been whiles I've been real mad because you weren't a lad. Ay, well, I've lived to see the folly o' my ways, and to thank God I'd nobbut a lass! You're worth a dozen Geordie Thornthets, any day o' the week. . . .'

She was gone with an answering smile directly he finished his speech, and the sound of her feet was light and swift on the stair. Hearing her, he, too, seemed to see her a girl again, gone to meet Geordie Thornthwaite along the shore. But instead of reviving and cheering him, it made him sad. He was too near the end to wish himself back at the start. He glanced at the lamp on the table to make sure that it was filled, and settled himself down to his papers with a sigh.

II

MAY stopped to speak to the hired girl as she went out, and was alarmed by the creeping dusk already in the inn. She breathed again when she was in the road, and saw the dull light holding yet on either hand. The soft closing of the door behind her gave her a long-forgotten thrill, bringing back similar autumn-evening hours, when she had gone to meet a lover from over the sands.

She got down to the shore about the time that the scene at Blindbeck was drawing to an end. She hurried, not only because she had little or no time to waste, but because she could not have gone slowly, if she had tried. The young May had never gone slowly, who was all kindness and knew nothing of pride. She ran down the shingle and across the sand, only pausing to draw breath and to reprove herself at the channel's edge. Passers-by on the flat road stopped to stare at her as she sped across, wondering what she could be doing, at that hour. Pausing, she looked across at the farm before she bent to the boat, chiding herself for her almost childish haste. But her tongue ached to let loose the words of persuasion that she carried with her, and her heart ached for the word of permission that she was sure she would carry back. She did not doubt for a

moment that Sarah would give way, so strong
was her inward belief that Geordie was coming
home.

At last she pushed off, stepped in and punted
herself across, and, once out again on dry ground,
tried to hold herself to a walk. The sand, ribbed
and hard beneath her feet, spoke to the fact that
the tide had been gone for hours. It was extraordinary how forgotten the sands always seemed
as soon as the tide had gone away. Only those
who had proved it by daily experience could
believe that the water would ever return. Even
to them it remained something of the miracle
that it was in truth, arousing continually a thrill
of awed surprise. Yet, side by side with that
impression of final retreat, of waste that had
always been waste and would never be reclaimed,
was one of a brooding terror that was only waiting its hour. The sea and the sands were like
cat and mouse, May thought—the one, aloof,
indifferent, yet always poised to leap; the other,
inert, paralysed though apparently free, and
always the certain victim in the end.

She looked behind and before from the quiet
home which she had left to the still more lonely
and quiet house which was her goal. There was
a point about half-way across at which it seemed
as if she would never reach the one, never get
back to the other in all time. Both seemed to
recede from her equally as she moved; vague
shapes formed only of imagination and the mist.
Just for a moment that vagueness of things which
she knew to be concrete caught her by the throat.
The little that she could see of the earth was so
cloud-like, so lacking in sturdy strength. The

very shore of the marsh looked as though a breath
might dissolve it in thin air. Though the distance
across was little more than a mile, the feeling of
space around her was infinite as the sky. The
sands seemed suddenly to become a treadmill
under her feet, turning and turning, but never
bringing her to the horizon which she sought.
The whole doorway of the bay was blocked by
the great wall of mist, and over the Lake mountains there was a smother of mist, and mist over
all the land that went east to the Pennine Range.
She began to fear even the crinkled sand which
felt so firm, as if it might suddenly sway and shift
like one of the many traps with which the bay
was sown. Behind her, the grey, faint-gleaming
strip of the channel seemed to cut her off from
her safe home. A slice of the bank broke suddenly
with an echoing splash, chilling her with the
lonely terror of water that has a victim in its hold.
The boat, helpless-looking, inert, a mere black
speck on the channel edge, seemed the only
insoluble thing beside herself. She longed for the
comfort of her feet on the tarred boards, for
the reassurance of her hands against the sculls. It
was a moment or two before she had the courage
to let it go, and face a world that was full of
bodiless shapes and evanescent shores.

But almost before she knew it she was on the
opposite side, scrambling up the stones to the
grassy slope beyond, and so, panting and hurrying, to the top of the sea-wall. She saw at once
that there was nobody in the house, that it was
still with the growing stillness of augmented
hours, and a further chill fell on her happy mood.
Yet she was glad at least to be there to welcome

the old folks when they came, and in any case they could not be very far. Every jolt of the trap must be bringing them nearer to the net which she was spreading so lovingly for their feet. They would be tired, of course, and probably very cross, but May was used to market-day moods and would not care. With affectionate ruthlessness she told herself that they would yield to her all the sooner for being tired. Presently they would agree unwillingly that she might have her way, and then she would hurry home again as if on wings. They would be crosser than ever after she had gone, vexed both with her and themselves and terribly touched in their pride. And then, slowly but surely, the hope that she had forced upon them would begin to race its stimulant through their veins. They would lie down to sleep with a secret gladness that they had not the courage to confess, and would wake in the morning and know that the world had been made for them anew.

She kept stopping the rush of her thoughts to send her senses over the marsh, but no sign of life came back to her, or sound of wheel or hoof. The wide stretches of grass and plough and the long length of road seemed almost as unsuggestive of human influence as the sands themselves. Swifter and swifter faded the passionate confidence which had sent her out, leaving the risks of the matter uppermost in her mind. She remembered that it was possible to be patient all one's life, and yet to wreck the fruits of it in an unguarded hour. This sudden mental and physical rashness might be symbolical of a greater rashness of the soul. Perhaps after to-night all her footholds and anchorages might go, leaving the world that she had managed so bravely only a nightmare blurred by tears.

The dusk thickened about her as the night tried to impress itself on the earth as a separate entity from the mist. The most that it could do, however, was to produce the effect of a hovering shadow from some huge, arrested wing. The real warning of night was in the deepened sense of loneliness and dread; of personal diminution in a growing space, in the further recession of things unseen as well as seen. It lay, too, in the stirring consciousness of the impending advent of the tide. She began to look anxiously towards her father's window for the lamp, and though she was comforted when she saw no sign, it stamped the illusion of desolation on her mind. Then she heard the cattle stir in the shippon as she walked along the wall, and was cheered and companioned by them for a little while. She would have gone down to them, or to the dog, who was always a firm friend, but she was afraid of losing her consciousness of time. She could not tear herself, either, from her breathless waiting for the silence to fill with life. She was cold whether she stood or walked, and more and more oppressed by a sense of folly and grave doubt. She even laughed at the middle-aged woman who had thrilled like a girl, but she laughed between her tears. Once or twice she ran down the bank and on to the sand, but always something drew her back; and at last, when she had listened so long that she had ceased to hear, there came the crunching sound of the Thornthwaite wheels. It was there suddenly where there had been no sign, as if it had only begun at the moment it reached her ear. At once her courage sprang up again, and her spirits rose. The whole affair was sweet and brave, once more. It was as if she had heard her lover himself coming surely towards her over the lonely marsh. . . .

III

SIMON uttered an exclamation when he saw the figure on the wall. His heart leaped first with a supernatural fear, and then with a sudden foreboding of some normal ill. His nerves were still unstrung from his experience with the car, and ready enough to shape familiar objects into ghosts. Even when he had recognised May and spoken her name, he could not rid himself of his feeling of alarm.

So he was not pleased to see her when she came running down; and Sarah, who had spent so kindly a morning with her, was not pleased, either. In the last few miles she had seemed to travel out of human touch, and there was a jar in the sudden intrusion of even this one thing left to her to love. Her brow contracted both with the effort of thought and the effort of sight, but indeed she knew well enough why May was there. Her intuition had worked uncertainly all the day, but it warned her now. She knew what impulse had brought May out to await their coming home.

Simon, however, had no clue to this sudden appearance at his journey's end. He sat still in the trap as she came swiftly through the yard, and then leaned out to address her with an anxious frown.

'Nay, now! Whatever's brought you trapesin'

here so late? Nowt wrong, is there? Father
badly again? Is he axin' for me, by any chance?'

She reassured him with a shake of the head
and a smile, and, as in the case of Mr. Dent, he
felt a sudden resentment towards smiles. In all
his life Simon had never encountered so many
smiling faces as had looked at him, that day.

'All's right, thank you. . . . Father's much
about the same. I wanted a word with Mrs.
Thornthet, that was all.

'You've been a terble while on the road,
though!' she added gaily, before he could speak.
'I'd about made up my mind as I'd have to be
getting back.'

'We were kept at Blindbeck, that's how it was,'
Simon said, remembering suddenly and with
gloom the precise circumstances in which they
had been kept. 'But if you nobbut wanted a
word wi' the missis, you could surely ha' waited
while morn. It's a daft-like trick to be lakin' on
t'sands when it's getting dark.'

His words made her turn again to throw a
glance at the inn, but still there was no summon-
ing gleam from the room upstairs. 'Ay, but tide
isn't till six,' she answered him coaxingly, turning
back, 'and I shan't be long. Father'll show a
light for me when it's time I was setting off.'

Sarah, ignoring the pair of them, had already
clambered out, and Simon remembered that he
had the horse to stable and the cows to milk and
feed. 'Danged foolishness, that's what it is!' he
growled, as he scrambled down, giving May a
very unaccustomed scowl. 'If I did as I should,
I'd be skifting you pretty sharp. Say what you've
gitten to say, and then clear out!'

Sarah had been moving away from them towards the house, but, as May followed her, she swung about. There was no invitation, however, in her rigid face.

'You've nowt to say as I know on,' she said in a curt tone, 'and I'm rarely tired. Anyway, there's no sense in lossing yourself for a bit of a chat.'

'I'll not lose myself, not I!' May laughed, advancing towards her, full of kindly warmth. She had been prepared for some such reception as this, and was not depressed. 'What, I've been across that often, it's the same to me as the road! I've been over when it was snowing—ay, and by moonlight, too. As for Geordie,' she added, with a tender laugh, 'he's crossed in the pitch dark, with only his nose to tell him where he was at!

'I was bound to ask you again before I slept,' she urged, casting a glance at Simon, busy with the horse. 'Can't I come in a minute?—I won't be long. It's late to be telling my business in the yard.'

'You've no business wi' me,' Sarah said stolidly, 'so you can stop off yon weam voice. You're not coming into Sandholes to-night, May Fleming, so that's flat!'

May laughed again, but there was less confidence in the laugh. She waited to speak again until Simon had moved away, the dog leaping and barking under the horse's nose.

'It's a shame,' she said cheerfully, 'to bother you so late, but I just couldn't bring myself to wait. It was you as brought it all back, Mrs. Thornthet, come to that, with yon talk at the doctor's of Geordie coming home!'

'There's no talk of him coming,' Sarah said coldly, 'and never was.' With one magnificent sweep she disposed of the fallacy of the afternoon. 'You ought to ha' more sense than to go fancying things like yon!'

'But you'd a letter, you said, begging his fare!' May was slightly bewildered, but went pressing on. 'You said he was keen to come, if he had the brass.'

'Ay, and there wasn't no brass; so yon's finished and by wi',' Sarah said.

'Ay, but there is,' May pleaded. 'Plenty o' brass!' She faltered a little before the other's lack of response. 'Nay, Mrs. Thornthet, don't you look like that! What does it matter where it comes from, if it makes folks glad?'

'I'll buy no gladness o' mine from *you*, my lass, as I said before.'

'I can spare the brass right enough—if it's only that.'

'Ay, but I can't spare the pride to take it,' Sarah said.

'Ay, well, then, think as you're buying *my* happiness!' May begged. 'I'd be real proud to think as I'd brought him back, even if he never looked aside at me again.'

'You'd have lile or nowt to be proud on, I'll be bound!' There was a touch of weary impatience in Sarah's voice. 'And what-like happiness would it be for you, in the end? Nay, May, my girl, we've thrashed the matter out, and I'm over-tired to be fret wi' it to-night.'

May sighed, and stood looking at her with troubled eyes, but she was unable to let the whole of her hope go.

'I'm right sorry to have put you about,' she said sadly. 'It's a real shame! Can't you promise to think it over a bit? I'll come over to-morrow for another talk.'

'I want neither talking nor thinking, so that's flat!' Sarah snapped. 'I'll promise to turn key in the door when I see you coming, and that's all!'

The tears came into May's eyes.

'You've no call to go telling me off like that,' she said, with a little break in her voice. 'I haven't done anything that's wrong, I'm sure.'

'You've shoved your nose into other folks' business,' Sarah said roughly—'that's what you've done! I'll thank you to leave us to do for our lad as'll suit us best!'

'He was mine, too!' May flung at her suddenly, roused at last. 'Long ago, maybe—years on years—but he was mine as well!'

Sarah gave a sneering laugh.

'There'll be more than one lass, I reckon, setting up to think that!'

May uttered a little cry, wounded to the heart.

'Eh, but you're a cruel woman, Mrs. Thornthet!' she exclaimed, in a voice quivering with pain. 'It's true I'd be glad to see Geordie again, but it don't make that much difference now. It's for your sake and poor Mr. Thornthet's that I want to see him back. . . .

'You're fond o' me, nowadays,' she went on bravely, controlling herself again. 'You like me well enough now, whatever you felt once. Can't you take the money for the sake of bygone times?'

But already Sarah had turned away from her and was moving towards the door. She fitted the

key in the lock with the ease of use, and gave the
rickety door an opening push. And again May
followed and stood, strong in the courage of those
who plead for the thing that they have at heart.

'Don't go away feeling mad with me, Mrs.
Thornthet!' she begged. 'I'm sorry I spoke as I
did. Think on how happy we were together, this
morning, you and me. Think how it would be if
he was to come marching into the yard. . . .'

Sarah was now over the threshold, with her
hand against the door, but May's hand was also
against it, refusing to let it close. Her face was
white as a flower upon the dusky air, pleading
and sweet with frank lips and tearful eyes. Sarah
herself was engulfed by the dark house, a shadow
that was yet more surely a block than the actual
door. It seemed to May that she had all the
passionless resistance of some ancient, immovable
stone. A lantern across showed the black squares
of the shippon stalls, the white coats of the beasts
and Simon moving from dark to light. May did
not know that the old woman's purpose was
giving in the pause, that that last sentence of
hers had broken the stubborn will. She waited
despairingly, seeking for more to say, and finding
nothing, since the right word had been said.
And because she despaired she broke the pause
too soon, in an access of hopelessness flinging
away her chance. Taking her hand from the
door, she pointed to Simon at his job.

'I'll ask Mr. Thornthet, then!' she cried
sharply, beginning to move away. 'Happen he'll
see to it for me instead of you. Happen he'll see
the offer's kindly meant, and not let pride and
such-like stand between!'

But Sarah, too, cried out before she had gone a yard, her voice harsh with wrath and a sort of fear.

'You leave Simon be,' she cried fiercely—'let him be! I've had enough o' your worry, without plaguin' him an' all. You get back to your dad, and don't come interfering again. You came between me and my lad, but you shan't meddle wi' my man! You mean well enough, I don't doubt, but you're nobbut a meddler, all the same. It never does to go shoving kindnesses at folk who keep on saying nay. If you force 'em, you do 'em more harm than good in the long run, by a deal. D'you think I want Geordie coming back in rags, as like a tramp on t'roads as a couple o' peas? D'you think I want a drunken do-nowt loafing about t'spot—a thief, maybe, or happen summat worse? What sort o' food and drink would yon be to Blindbeck, d'you think? Eliza's gitten enough on her tongue, without the likes o' that! Nay, the lad as went was a limb, and he was bonny and smart, and Eliza'll always think of him like yon. She'll always think in her heart as he was the better o' Jim, for all she talks so loud. But if he come back to shame us, it'd rob me even o' that. I couldn't abide it!' she finished vehemently. 'It'd be worse than death. I'd rather the sea took him afore ever he reached home!'

She stopped with an indrawn breath, and the door, creaking abruptly, showed that her weight was heavy on the latch. May stood still in the yard, as still as the shadow that had once again turned to ancient stone. The silence that had fallen between them seemed to push her away, to drive them so far apart that never again would they be able to speak. At last, in that terrible outpouring, May had discovered the real barrier to her desire. There were pride and generosity in the way, but there was also something which she could not fight. The monstrous, lifelong obsession of Eliza had stopped even the natural road to a mother's heart.

Fear came over her, a more terrible fear than had taken her on the sands. In the quiet spot that should have been homely because of the moving light and the dumb beasts, she had a hint of something not quite sane. Things that had no place in the life of the soil seemed suddenly to have forced a passage in. She peered into the darkness of Sarah's mind, as her bodily eyes sought for her hidden face.

She was startled into action again by the old dog's nose thrust kindly into her hand. He had listened to the urgent voices with constantly-pricked ears, knowing by instinct that somebody suffered and was afraid. Now he came to May, begging her to take charge of her soul, lest he, too, whose only trust was in Man, should suffer fear. She laid her hand for a moment on the warmth of his head, dropping her gaze to meet his upturned eyes. Instantly, however, as if he had brought her a further message, she looked towards the bay, and saw the lamp in her father's window spring to life.

She was loath to go with this wreck of things at her feet, but in her destitution of heart she was afraid to stay. Armed with the promise, she would have cared nothing for dark or tide, but with this weight at her heart it seemed as if it

would take her all the night to cross the sand.
She tried to believe that she would return to
wrestle with Sarah in the day, but she knew well
enough that she would never return. Eliza, and
all that Eliza had meant in their spoiled lives,
lay like a poisonous snake across her path.

She wondered drearily what had become of
the passionate certainty with which she had set
out. The sea still sundered her lover and herself,
the bar of the sea so much greater than any
possible stretch of land. There were people to
whom the sea was a sort of curse, and perhaps,
without knowing it, she was one of those. She
loved it, indeed, but she never forgot that it had
taken her first hope. Perhaps it mocked at her
love as Sarah had mocked her love. Perhaps
it was only waiting out in the dark to do her
harm. . . .

She made one last entreating movement towards the shadow that was stone, but nobody
moved in the darkness and nobody spoke. She
could not be sure at that moment whether Sarah
was there, or whether all that she begged of
was merely blackened space. Then she began
by degrees to move away, wrenching her feet,
as it were, from the ground of the yard. Sadly,
without looking back, she mounted the sea-wall,
bowed by her burden of failure and sorrow and
self-contempt. But the fear took her again as soon
as she faced the sands, and she hurried down the
farther side. The good angel of the Thornthwaites fled away into the night as if driven
by flails.

GEORDIE-AN'-JIM

I

THE blackness stirred in the doorway and became human again, setting the door to the jamb with a firm, decisive push. Sarah followed the dark stone passage to the kitchen, moving with freedom on the ground she knew. In the bare, silent room, that seemed at the same time barer and yet more peopled because of the dusk, she took off her old mantle, her shabby bonnet, and her black thread gloves. She set a lighted candle on the table in the middle of the room, and from the cupboard by the hearth she took paper and wood, and kindled a pale, unhomely glow in the dusty, ash-filled grate. In the outer darkness that was the scullery she filled the kettle, and brought it to wait the reluctant patronage of the fire. It was not yet night over the sands, but the candle was more than sufficient to quench the fainting effort of the day. The only outside light was the steady glow of the lamp, set in the face of the inn to call its daughter home.

Still, however, the house seemed unaroused, and would remain so until the master came in, because those who live much by themselves do not hear the sound of their own feet. They seem to themselves to move like ghosts through the rooms; it is only their thoughts that they hear about the place. And there are no houses so quiet as those which spend half their days hearkening to that eternal talker, the sea. The other half of their lives is still as the sands are still, sharing that same impression of quittance for all time.

The kitchen, once perfectly kept, was already beginning to show signs of Sarah's failing sight. There were holes in the cloth rug which she unrolled before the fire, and slits in the patchwork cushions on the rush-bottomed chairs. The pots in the half-empty pot-rail were all askew, and the battered pewter and brass had ceased to put in its claim to be silver and gold. There was an out-of-date almanac under the old clock, and an ancient tide-table over the mantelshelf. But the real tragedy of the place was not in its poverty but in its soul. Behind the lack of material comfort there was a deeper penury still—the lack of hope and a forward outlook and a reason for going on. The place was cold because the hearts of its tenants were growing cold.

The candle, as always, drove the impression of utter desolation home. No other light produces that same effect of a helpless battle against the dark. No other is so surely a symbol of the defiant human soul, thinking it shines on the vast mysteries of space. No other shows so clearly the fear of the soul that yet calls its fear by the name of courage and stands straight, and in the midst of the sea of the dark cries to all men to behold that courage and take heart.

All about that little challenge of light were the brooding obscurities of sand and marsh, and, nearer yet, the looming enigma of the empty house. At the back of the mind there was always the consciousness of unlit rooms, of echoing passages, and climbing, creaking stairs. Always at night there is that mystery of terror in a half-used house, pressing on those who crouch in some charmed corner of its walls.

Sarah was different, somehow, now that she was at home, and free of the outdoor clothes which she had worn all day. It was as if bonnet and mantle were the armour of her class, in which she was ready to face the offensive of the world. Without it she was more primitive and more human, relaxed in muscles and nerves. Now one could guess at the motherliness in her to which Jim had clung, unswervingly trusting in spite of her dislike. Her grey hair had been slightly ruffled both by the bonnet and the drive, and on her old neck it even curled a little, showing itself still soft and fine.

She was tired with that terrible tiredness which sees the day behind like a series of folding cardboard views. She seemed to have lived many days in that single day, with never a moment between them to fit her for the next. More than once, indeed, she had been ready to collapse, but always the stimulus of some fresh event had set her going again. Now she had reached the point when she was too tired to allow herself to be tired; when body and mind, usually careful to save the next day's strength, recklessly lay both hands upon their all.

Even at the last moment had come the sudden struggle with May, and the zest of that strife still tingled in her veins. After that long day of damaged pride it was pleasant to have asserted it in the end, to have claimed the right to suffer rather than be forcibly blessed. All day she had tasted in prospect the salt·savour of another's bread, but here was something that she could refuse. She was still too stiff with fight to care that she had wounded a generous nature in the act. It was true that she could not have borne the sight of a Geordie who would have brought her fresh disgrace. The love that cares for the broken more than the sound could not thrive while she feared the sneer of the idol to whom she would not bow.

Beyond, in the dairy, there came the sound of metalled boots, and the pails spoke musically on the flags as Simon set them down. She heard him shuffling across to open the inner door, and then—'Milk's in, missis!' he called to her, as his head came through.

There was a nervous sound in his voice, at which Sarah almost smiled, knowing that his conscience must be ill at ease. She answered 'Oh, ay,' without turning, for she was busy with the fire, which, as if hating the atmosphere into which it was born, was doing its best to escape from it again.

'I'll see to the fire for you, missis,' he said, crossing to her side. 'Set you down and be easy a bit. You're likely tired.'

'Nay, I'll manage all right,' she protested stolidly, and then suddenly yielded to him, and moved away. She did not sit down, however, but remained standing on the hearth, while he went on his knees to set the bellows between the bars.

'May give me a fair start,' he observed presently, when the flame had consented to grow. 'What was she after, coming off like that?'

'Nay, it was nowt much,' Sarah said easily, in an indifferent tone. 'It was nobbut some daftness she'd got in her head, that's all.'

'She mun ha' been rarely keen to come across

so late. Was it summat or other she wanted you to do?'

'Ay,' Sarah said firmly, 'but I couldn't see my way. I tellt her so this morning when I see her in town.'

'Summat about your eyes, likely?' he enquired nervously, blowing hard.

'Losh save us, no! It was nowt to do wi' that.'

'Will was rarely put out when I tellt him what doctor had said,' Simon went on. 'He was right sorry, he was, and real anxious to do what he could.'

'Ay, he's kind, is Will. He's a right good friend. But I won't take owt I can help from him, all the same.'

'Because o' yon woman of his?' Simon asked angrily, stumbling to his feet. He threw a last glance at the fire, and saw that it seemed resigned to its now evident fate. He was sorry for Sarah, and guiltily conscious of his own relief, but the thought of Eliza whipped his mind to rage. This was nothing new, though, either to man or wife, after the usual meeting at the end of the week. However long they had held their tongues from her name, it was suddenly out, and the air was vibrating at once with the rising tremolo of their hate.

'Nay, then, what's yon besom to do wi' it, any way round? Will's money's his own, I reckon, and he can do as he likes. Happen you'll choose to see sense about it come Judgment Day, but not afore!'

'A farmer's wife addles half his brass—we all know that. You can't touch a man wi'out laying a finger on his folks.'

'A deal Eliza's done for him,' Simon scoffed, 'barrin' giving him best of her tongue! I'll be bound you'd never think twice about t'brass if you and Eliza was friends. It's this spite as there is atween you as sets you taking things amiss. Eliza would likely ha' been no worse than most, if you hadn't made sure she was always wanting a slap!'

Sarah received these remarks with an ironic smile.

'Bosom friends we'd ha' been, d'ye think,' she asked, 'if I'd nobbut seen my way to a bit more care?'

'Nay, well, I wouldn't be sure about that,' he returned grandly, hedging with ease. 'But we'd all ha' done better, I'll take my oath, if you hadn't been that smart to take offence.'

'Happen I'd ha' done best to hold my tongue, when she was telling all Witham we'd gitten notice to quit?'

'Nay, I don't know about that!' ... He was stamping about the floor. 'A bit o' tact wi' her, happen? ... nay, dang her, I don't know!' ... Leastways, you needn't ha' tellt her yon rubbish, this afternoon,' he concluded, brought to a stand.

'You'd have had me set by and say nowt while she sneered at our lad?'

'Nay, then, I wouldn't—dang her! ... I wouldn't, that's flat!'

'You'd have had me say nowt, neither, yon day we was wed—give her a kiss, happen, and praise her gown——?'

Nay, then, I wouldn't, I tell you! Blast you! Nowt o' the sort!' Simon was fairly shouting now. He thumped at the table in his rage. 'I wish to gox I could ha' gitten my hands round her throat wi'out having to swing!'

Sarah looked at his prancing shape with the same ironic smile.

'Nay, my lad, there's better ways than that wi' Eliza, by a deal. D'ye think I haven't gitten a bit o' my own back, now and then? I've had my knife in her deep—ay, deep!—time and again. There's better ways wi' Eliza than just twisting her neck. What, this very day I've made her weep tears as she's never wept afore—tears as near tears o' blood as Eliza'll ever weep. . . .' She stopped, recalling the scene in which nature had shone like a star in Eliza just for once. . . . 'Nay, Simon,' she went on quietly, 'there's no sense in our getting mad. It's over late to go preaching love atween Eliza and me. Men don't know what hate can be between women when it's gitten hold. It's a thing best let alone—never mentioned—let alone. It's a big thing, caged-like, as was small once, and then comes full-grown. It's over late to go trying to stroke it through the bars.'

'I nobbut wanted to make the best o' things,' Simon muttered, ashamed. 'The Lord knows I'd give my hand to put you top-dog of Eliza just for once. But I'm not denying I'm terble thankful to ha' fixed things up. I reckon I'll sleep to-night as I haven't for weeks. I'm right sorry, though, if you're taking it hard.'

'I'll take it right enough when it's here,' Sarah said gently, turning away. 'I won't make no bother about it, don't you fret.'

She picked up the kettle and set it on the fire, as if she meant to put an end to the talk. Simon lingered, however, casting uneasy glances at her face.

'I've a job in t'far shippon to see to,' he said at last, and lighted the old lantern that swung against the wall. . . . 'Yon's tide, surely?' he added suddenly, as he took it down. . . . 'Nay, it's over soon.'

He lifted the lantern to look at the table above the shelf, but Sarah shook her head.

'Yon's an old table, think on. It's no use looking there. Tide's six o'clock, if you want to know.'

He said, 'Oh, ay. I'd clean forgot,' and still stood on the hearth, as if reluctant to go. Presently he spoke humbly, twisting the lantern in his hand.

'It's real hard on you, Sarah, to come down like this. I don't know as I like it, myself, but it's worse for you. But we've been right kind wi' each other all these years. You'll not think shame on me when I'm a hired man?'

She turned back to him, then, trying to see his face, and it seemed to him that she really saw him for the first time in many months. But, in point of fact, it was the eyes of the mind that were looking at the eyes of the mind. . . . And then, unexpectedly, he saw her smile.

'Nay, my lad,' she said strongly, 'you mun be wrong in t'garrets to think that! If there's owt to think shame on, it'll be stuff like yon. You're the same lad to me as when we was wed, just as Eliza's the same cruel, jibing lass. I reckon that's where the trouble lies, if it come to that. Love and hate don't change, neither on 'em, all our lives. D'you think I'd ha' kept my hate so warm if I hadn't ha' kept love?'

He nodded doubtfully in reply, and began slowly to edge away. But before he had reached the threshold he paused again.

'Anyway, we've had the best on't!' he cried triumphantly, as if inspired. 'Eliza's had what looks most, but we've had the real things, you and me!' And then, as she did not speak, the spirit died in him, and his head drooped. 'Ay, well, we mun do what we can,' he finished lamely. 'We mun do what we can. 'Tisn't as if it'll be so long for either on us, after all.'

'Shall I see to t'milk for you?' he added diffidently, but was refused.

'Nay,' Sarah said. 'I can manage right well. I know they milk-pans better than my face. I'd like to stick to my job as long as I can.'

Simon said, 'Ay, well, then, I'll be off!' and looked at the door; and stared at the door, and said, 'Ay, well, I'll be off!' again. He had an uneasy feeling that he ought to stay, but there was that job in the far shippon he wanted to do. He wandered uncertainly towards the outer door, and then, almost as if the door had pushed him, stumbled into the yard.

II

SARAH stood thinking after Simon had gone, following with ease the troubled workings of his mind. The smile came back to her lips as she recalled his obvious sense of guilt. Behind all his anger and chafing humiliation it was easy to see his growing pleasure and relief. It was more than likely, indeed, that he would be priding himself on his new position before so long. Perhaps age, which has a merciful as well as a cruel blindness

of its own, might prevent him from ever realising
where he stood. She could picture him lording it
over the gentler-natured Will, and even coming
in time to dominate the farm. It was only for her
that there would be no lording it—and open
sight. It was only on her account that he was
still ashamed.

It was cruel to grudge him the little solace
he had left, but the thing which eased the position for him would form a double cross for her.
Hitherto, they had stood together in their hatred
of Blindbeck and its female head, and in the very
depth of their darkness still had each other to
soothe their shame. But now Simon's attitude
was bound to alter at least towards the farm.
There would come a day when he would turn
upon her for some chance remark, and from that
hour he would be openly on Blindbeck's side.
The new tie would make him forget those bitter
upheavals of jealous rage. Slowly the place
would come between them until she was left to
hate alone.

For her, the change would simply deliver her,
blind and bound, into Eliza's hand. She could
have laughed as she saw how the thing she had
fought against all her life had captured her at
last. Even with Eliza dead or gone, Blindbeck
would still have stifled her as with unbreathable
air. Her spirit and Eliza's would have lived their
battles again, and even over a grave she would
have suffered and struggled afresh. But Eliza
was neither dead nor mercifully removed, but
was already snuffing the battle-smoke from afar.
The whole account of their lives would come up
in full, and be settled against the under-dog for

good. It was as whipping-boy to Eliza that she would go to the house by Blindbeck gates.

At the present moment, however, she neither suffered nor rebelled. Physically, she had reached the point at which the mind detaches itself resolutely from further emotional strain. The flame of hate burnt steadily but without effort, and with almost as pure a light as the flame of love itself. Like all great passions, it lifted her out of herself, lending her for the time being a still, majestic strength. There is little to choose at the farthest point of all between the exaltation of holiness and the pure ecstasy of hate. To the outside eye they show the same shining serenity, almost the same air of smiling peace. It is the strangest quality in the strange character of this peculiarly self-destroying sin. Because of it she was able to go about her evening tasks with ease, to speak gently to Simon in the little scene which had just passed, and even to dwell on his methods with a tolerant smile upon her lips.

In the clarified state of her mind pictures rose sharply before her, covering all the years, yet remaining aloof as pictures, and never stirring her pulse. So clear they were that they might have been splashed on the canvas that instant with a new-filled brush. They sprang into being as a group springs under the white circle of a lamp, as the scenes the alive and lit brain makes for itself on the dark curtain of the night. The few journeys she had taken in life she travelled over again—rare visits to Lancashire and Yorkshire . . . Grasmere . . . Brough Hill Fair. They had stayed in her mind because of the slow means by which they were achieved, but they counted for very little in the tale of things. It is not of these casual experiences that the countryman thinks when the time comes for a steady reviewing of his life; that intent, fascinated returning upon tracks which is the soul's preparation for the next great change. They flit to and fro, indeed, like exotic birds against a landscape with which they have nothing to do, but it is the landscape itself which holds the eye, and from which comes the great, silent magic that is called memory, and mostly means youth. It is the little events of everyday life that obsess a man at the last; the commonplace, circular come-and-go that runs between the cradle and the grave. Not public health problems, or new inventions, or even the upheavals of great wars; but marriage, birth and death, the coming of strangers destined to be friends, the changing of tenants in houses which mean so much more than they ever mean themselves. Binding all is the rich thread of the seasons, with its many-coloured strands; and, backing all, the increasing knowledge of Nature and her ways, that revolving wheel of beauty growing ever more complex and yet more clear, more splendid and yet more simple as the pulses slow to a close.

She loved the plain, beautiful farming life that a man may take up in his hand because it is all of a piece, and see the links of the chain run even from end to end. Even now she could see the fair-haired child she had been still running about her home, the child that we all of us leave behind us in our sacred place. She could hear the clatter of clogs in her father's yard, and all about her the sound of voices which the daisied earth had stopped. It was strange, when she came to think of it, that she never heard her own. In all her memories of the child it seemed to her lip-locked, listening and dumb. Perhaps it was because she was shut in the child's brain that she could not hear it speak. She could hear her mother's voice, light and a little sharp, and her father's a deep rumble in a beard. Even in the swift pictures flashing by her he looked slow, drifting with steady purpose from house to farm. Because of his slowness he seemed to her more alive than his wife; there was more time, somehow, to look at him as he passed. Her bustling, energetic mother had become little more than a voice, while the seldom-speaking man was a vital impression that remained.

Rising up between the shadows that blotted them out was a certain old woolly sheep-dog and the red torch of the flowering currant beside the door. There was also a nook in the curve of the garden wall, where, under a young moon, she had seen the cattle coming across the fields, sunk to their horns in a fairy-silver mist. . . .

It was an open-air life that took her long miles to school, clogging on frozen roads, through slanting rain or fighting against the wind. School itself seemed patched in a rather meaningless fashion on that life, much as the books in the parlour on the busy, unthinking house. A life of constant and steadily-increasing work, from errands of all sorts, feeding the hens and fetching home the cows, to the heavier labour of washing and baking, milking, helping with the stock. Presently there had been the excitement of the first shy dance, and then the gradual drawing towards marriage as the tide draws to the moon.

And all the time there had been Eliza making part of her life, from the plump little girl whom people stopped to admire to the bold intruder at the altar-rail. Looking back, she could see herself as a stiff and grave-eyed child, grimly regarding the round-faced giggler from the start. Even then she had always been the dumb man in the stocks, of whom the street-urchin that was Eliza made mock as she danced and played. Only once had she ever definitely got the better of her, and it had had to last her all her life. Eliza had had many lovers, drawn by the counterfeit kindliness which hid her callous soul, but when she had chosen, at last, it was Simon who was her choice. Perhaps the one gleam of romance in Eliza's life had been when she looked at Simon . . . and Simon had looked away. Quite early he had fixed his affections on Sarah, and during their long courtship he had never swerved. Plain, businesslike Sarah had drawn him after her as the moon draws the willing tide. . . .

She began to put away the things she had bought in Witham, stowing them in a cupboard between the pot-rail and the door. During the morning she had felt royally that she was buying half the town, but now she saw how small her share of the marketing had been. There was a troubled feeling at the back of her mind that something had been missed, and even though she was sure of her purchases, she counted them again. Afterwards, she stood muttering worriedly through the list . . . tea, candles, a reel of cotton . . . and the rest. And then, suddenly, without any help from the candles and cotton, she remembered what it was, and smiled at the childish memory that would not stay asleep.

More than twenty years, she reminded herself —and yet she still looked for the fairing that Geordie had brought her on Martinmas Day! There had scarcely been any special season— Christmas, Whitsun, Easter or Mid-Lent—but he had remembered to mark it by some frolicsome gift. He had always withheld it from her until the last, and then had stood by her laughing while she unwrapped some foolish monkey on dancing wires. All the time he was saying how splendid the fairing was going to be—'It's gold, mother, real gold—as bright as the King's crown!' And when she had opened it, she would pretend to be cast down, and then put it snugly away and say it was 'real grand!'

Jim had had his fairings for her, too, but she was trying her very hardest not to remember those. Jim's had been prettier and more thoughtful—often of real use, but she had long since forgotten what the things were like. A mug with her name on it, a handkerchief, a brooch—long ago broken or lost, or even given away. But every ridiculous object of Geordie's was under lock and key, with even a bit of camphor to keep the monkey from the moth. . . .

She stood there smiling, softly folding her hands, as if she laid them lightly over some sudden gift. On either side of her was a laughing face, and even she found it hard to tell which was which. She was very still as she made that perfect transition into the past, and the only sound in her ears was through the lips that laughed. And

then, into that full stillness, in which no step
moved or voice called or bird flew, there came
the cry of a heron outside the door.

III

IT did not reach her at first. She heard it, indeed,
coming back to the present with the sound, but
that was all. The thing behind it had to travel
after her over twenty years. The cry of the
heron was natural enough, with a famous heronry
so near, and it was only because of the excep-
tional stillness of the night that it drew her attention now. Her mind went mechanically to the
high wood behind the Hall, to the long-necked,
slender-legged birds going home to the tall trees
that on this unstirred evening would be stiff as
a witch's broom. She even had time to remember
the old legend of their battle with the rooks,
before the thing that had been running for twenty
years entered her consciousness with a rush.

She stiffened, then. From being softly still she
became a rigid thing, stiller than sleep, stiller
than death, because it was passionate will-power
that held her still. It was already a moment or
two since the sound had passed, but it still rang
in the ear which had seemed to refuse to take it
in. It had flashed through her brain like a bright
sword flung in a high arc through a night without
a star, but the truth that was behind it she held
rigidly from her, even as it tried to step within.
She knew that it was too low for a bird's call, too
sharp and clear in that muffle of mist, but she
shut the knowledge out. She would not let herself either breathe or think until she had heard
the sound again.

The shock was as great, the second time, but it had a different effect. She began to tremble from head to foot; even her lips parted and shook; her hands relaxed and began to pluck at her gown. Her breath came in quick gasps that were almost sobs as her eyes strained towards the darkness that held the door. Her brain kept insisting to her body that it must be still, but it was too strong for it, and paid no heed. Her heart alone, beating in hard, ponderous strokes, seemed as if by itself it must shut out any further sound; and when the call came the third time, breaking the silence so that it could not close again, her own power of restraint went by the board, as well. Her hands lifted themselves and gripped each other across her breast, and her voice, shaken and full of tears, forced itself into her throat. 'Jim!' she heard herself saying, 'Jim!' —with no knowledge that she had meant to speak, and in that one word admitted the final defeat of all her life.

Then the knocking began, the terrible brazen knocking which soulless iron makes on the unresponsive door of an empty house. It was as if whoever knocked frightened himself by the knocking, and tried to beat away his fear with still louder blows. But to the woman who tried to pretend that the house was really empty it was more terrible still. It seemed to take on the sound of a summons to the soul itself to issue forth. The noise of it flooded the place, echoed its way upstairs and into far rooms, so that strange voices answered it sharply from wood and stone. The heavy, storm-tried walls were suddenly no more than paper, so that the knocking became folly when a push would have forced them in. It seemed to Sarah that they must hear it from end to end of the marsh, across at the 'Ship,' and out to the hidden edge of sea. She wondered why Simon did not come running, and the dog break into hoarse barks, for even in the far shippon they must surely hear. But there was only that great knocking in the world, cheerful, impatient, or resigned, by turn. It paused, at moments, but only as the passing-bell pauses, Sarah thought, waiting to speak its single word afresh.

The noise had swept away in a moment both the false serenity of hate and the almost falser calm of that dwelling memory of love. From the respite, indeed, the live passion seemed to have sunk, as it were, on its haunches for a fiercer leap. She could not think clearly or control her limbs under the sudden impact of its spring. It seemed to fling itself on her as she had seen the tides in the winter crash against the wall. She, too, went under as if the water had beaten her down, and the noise at the door became the blows of the waves and the roar of the dragged beach.

She had that impulse to laughter which comes with long-expected woe, as if the gods were guilty of bathos when they stooped at last to strike. Scorn is the first sensation of those who seem to have watched the springs of action long before the hour. Sudden sorrows, quick blows have a majesty of their own, as if the gifts of the gods made for honour in good or ill. But long-deferred trouble, like suspended joy, has a meaner quality in fulfilment, and a subtle humiliation in its ache. That when the gods come they come quickly is true for both libations from the emptied cup. Royal sorrows, like royal joys, fall swift as thunderbolts from heaven.

She had always known in her heart that there was no fighting Blindbeck luck; that even the dregs of it were more potent than the best of the Sandholes brand. It could hardly fail to reach even across the sea, so that one of the failures would be less of a failure than the other, in the end. The trouble of being the under-dog too long is that even the dog himself begins at last to think it his rightful place. For all her dreaming and lying on Geordie's behalf, she would have found it hard to believe in his ultimate success. Not for nothing had Eliza carefully tended her Method all this while, and watered it weekly with the Simons' tears.

At first she told herself that she would put out the light, and let the knocker knock until he was tired. Perhaps he would open the door and step inside, but the darkness would surely thrust him out again. He might even go to the foot of the stairs and call, until the silence itself put a hand upon his throat. But already the strain was more than she could bear, and each blow as it came was a blow on her own heart. She tried to move, but was afraid of the sound of her own feet, and it was only under the cover of fresh knocking that she made the effort at last. Now she was facing the door which she could not see, though she knew its panels like the palm of her hand. Behind it, she felt the knocking ring on her brain, but now she had come within range of a more persistent power than that. Plainly, through the wooden barrier that was raised between them, she felt the presence of the man who stood without.

There is always an effort, a faint dread, about the opening of a door, as if the one who entered were admitted to more than a room. From each personality that enters even for a moment into one's life something is always involuntarily received. The opening is only a symbol of the more subtle admission of the two, which leaves an intruder behind when the actual bodily presence has passed away. And of all openings there is none that includes such realisation and such risk as that which lets in the night and a stranger's face.

And then suddenly the knocking ceased, as if the knocker were now as aware of her presence as she of his. They were like enemies, crouched on either side of a barricade; or like lovers, so near and yet so far, in the last, long second before the bars are down. Each waited for a breath, a touch, a turn of the hand that would bring the flash of the final blow or the thrill of the first kiss.

Their consciousness of each other was so strong that she knew at once when he lifted his arm again, just as he knew when she stirred in fear of the fresh attack. The latch gave its loose, metallic clink as she raised it and let it drop, and then the door began to open with the almost human grudging of old doors. The stranger put out a hand to help it on its way, and, with a harsh shriek that sounded like protest, it dragged across the flags.

At once the bulk of his big form was in the open square, substantial even in the dissolving light. There was a last pause as the shock of the actual meeting smote upon their minds, and then his voice, cheerful and loud as the knocking, flooded the house.

'Everybody dead here?' he demanded gaily, bending forward to peer at the figure set like a statue just inside. The tone of his voice, deep and kindly, had yet a touch of nervousness at its back. The strain of the waiting had told upon him as well as on her. 'Say, you *are* real, ain't you?' he enquired sharply, and then laughed. 'Mercy! I sure thought everybody must be dead!'

Sarah had another shock at the sound of his voice, topped by the accent from over the pond as the deep note of flood is topped by the thinner note of the surf. She had listened instinctively for the Jim-an'-Geordie voice, but this was the voice of neither Geordie nor Jim. It was as strange to her who knew nothing of other peoples' speech as if it had been a voice from another star. She shrank away from him, saying, 'I thought it was Jim.' And then, almost violently, 'You're never Jim!'

The man laughed a second time, but more naturally, as if reassured, the moment he heard her speak. 'I sure am!' he answered her joyfully. 'Why shouldn't I be? Leastways, I'm all of Jim Thornthet that's managed to swim across!' The smile stayed on his lips as he stared, but died when she did not respond. 'May I come in a spell?' he enquired anxiously. 'I've only struck England to-day, and I've a bag of news.'

But again she blocked the entrance as she had blocked it for May. It was the way into herself as well as into the house that these people sought,

and she yielded to neither of them by an inch.
'You can get out, if you're Jim,' she said caustic-
ally, 'and as smart as you like! Blindbeck's your
spot. We want nowt wi' you here.'

The sharp words did not depress him, however. They were too reminiscent of old time.

'That's a real mean how-d'ye do!' he answered
her humorously, advancing a foot. ' 'Tisn't like
Westmorland folk to keep folk tugging at the
latch. . . . Shucks for Blindbeck!' he added
laughingly, as she began the word again. 'Sandholes is my little old home—always was, and
always will be.' He advanced farther, a merry,
teasing note in his big voice. 'You can't keep
me out, old woman! You never could. I'm coming right in, old woman! . . . I'm sure coming.
. . . I'm right in!'

It was true, too. He was in the passage now,
making his way by a force of desire stronger than
May's entreating love. Something else helped
him as well, perhaps—some old extorted freedom
of house and board. He put out his hand to
Sarah as he turned to the light, but she shrank
away from him against the wall.

'I won't have you in t'house!' she cried angrily
to his dim form. 'Be off with you now, and look
sharp about it!'

But again he seemed to be pleasantly cheered
by her wrath, as if with a happy echo from the
past.

'I'll shin off right quick when I've had a word,'
he coaxed. 'Come on in, old woman, and look
at me where there's a bit more sun!' The flicker-
ing light seemed to beckon him on, for he began
to move towards its dim dwelling. 'I've news of

Geordie for you,' he called back to her, as she did not stir. 'You'll sure be wanting to hear that!'

She heard him pass into the kitchen, his firm, confident tread raising a ring from every flag, and wondered, as with the knocking, why it did not carry all over the marsh. But still she stayed behind, fighting with herself and with the longing to hear his news. It could be of nothing but failure, she reminded herself, and her heart answered that that would be better than nothing at all. She heard him walking about the kitchen, as if he walked from this memory to that, peering into old cupboards and laying a hand upon old chairs. Presently, however, there came a silence as if he had seen enough, and, in a sudden panic lest he should be gone, she hurried after him into the room.

At once, as she went in, she traced the shape of him on the hearth, though she could not see his huge shadow that climbed the ceiling and swamped the wall. Clearly, too, she could feel his dominant personality all about, too heady a wine for the frail, cobwebbed bottle of the place. Paused on the hearth, he was still looking around him with a wistful, humorous smile. He was thinking, as all think who return, how strong and yet how slender was the chain, how futile and yet how tenacious were the humble things which had held him through the years! He was thinking, too, how amazingly tiny everything had grown—the house, the kitchen, and the old woman within the door. Even the stretch of sand, which he could vaguely see, seemed narrow to him who had known much greater wastes.

He turned his smiling eyes suddenly to Sarah's
face.

'How's the old man, by the way? Still keeping uppermost of the weeds?'

'He's nobbut middlin', that's all,' she forced
herself to reply.

'Is he anywhere about?'

'Like enough . . . but you needn't wait.'

'I'd like a chin with him, all the same!' He
hugged himself as he stood on the hearth, and his
huge shadow hugged itself on the wall. The same
mischievous sound crept back into his voice. 'I'm
mighty glad to see you again, old woman, I am
that! Perhaps you'll feel like slinging me a smile
or two after a bit.'

'Eliza'll smile, I'll warrant, if you've nobbut a
pound or two in your poke.'

'I have that—sure!' He slapped his coat as
he spoke, laughing a great laugh which shook
her as cruelly as his knock. 'It's up to me to
keep my pockets stitched, nowadays,' he finished,
in a contented tone.

'I'm main glad to hear it,' she said sardonically,
and he nodded gaily.

'That's real nice of you, old woman! You can
keep right on. You'd a terrible down on me in
the old days, hadn't you now?'

'I've no use for you, Jim Thornthwaite, and
never had. You know that as well as me.'

'That's so!' He laughed again. 'But I was
always mighty fond of *you*.' He made a movement as if to cross to her side, but she backed
instantly, as if she guessed. 'Of course, you'd a
deal rather it had been Geordie,' he said. 'I
know that. But he was never much of a sparkle

in the family tarara, and that's honest. I left
him serving in a store—poor lad Geordie—and
hankering like honey after the old spot!'

'And you left him behind,' Sarah flung at him
—'you wi' brass?'

'He wouldn't take a red cent. I looked him
up as soon as I struck it rich, but he was always
set on hoeing his own row. He'd have taken it
from his own folks, but he wouldn't from me.
Guess it was Blindbeck hate in him coming out
at last! But if ever he'd had the dollars, he'd
have been home before you could hear him
shout.'

'He's best where he is,' Sarah said coldly,
repenting her charge. Eliza's son should not
see that she grudged or cared. 'Them as makes
beds can likely lie on the straw.'

'Well, Blindbeck luck still holds, anyway!'
Jim smiled. 'See here!' He put his hand in
the great-coat that seemed to hide from her that
he was a creature of flesh and blood, and instantly
she heard the rustle of notes. He opened the big
pocket-book under the light, running his hand
over the clean slips with joyous pride. 'Don't
that talk?' he said cheerfully. 'Doesn't it sure
talk?' and in spite of her resolve she shrank from
the crisp, unaccustomed sound.

'Good enough, eh?' he demanded warmly—
'and there's plenty more behind! That's only
to pass the time o' day with, so to speak. Guess
it'll do for a fairing for my old mother, that's
about all.' He snapped the elastic again and
flung the book on the table, so that it slid across
within Sarah's reach. Lifting his eyes he met her
gaze fixed blindly upon his face, and his brow

contracted as he puzzled over that hard, unrecognising stare.

'Can't we sit down for a spell?' he asked her coaxingly, turning back to the hearth. 'I feel real unwanted, standing on my hind legs.'

'Eliza'll be waiting on you,' Sarah said, through a stiff throat.

'She's waited twenty years.' He laid a hand on a chair and pulled it nearer to the warmth. It protested violently when it felt his weight, but he settled himself snugly, and did not care. The fire, as if heartened at sight of him on the hearth, changed its cold yellow for a crimson glow.

'It's good to be home,' he said happily—'good as a Sunday-school treat—sure!' He pulled his pipe from his pocket, and began to fill it meditatively, with quiet hands. . . . 'Now, if it had been Geordie that had struck it rich, it would have been a real hum for you, wouldn't it, old woman? Guess I feel real mean, for your sake, that it's only me. Guess I could almost wish it was Geordie out and out!'

He leaned forward with the firelight on his face, looking at her with the same smile that was like a hand that he reached out.

'He was always making a song,' he said, 'about what he'd do when he struck it rich. "I'll be off home that slick you'll hear the bump," he used to say, "and I'll be planning all the way how I'll burn the cash! I'd like to buy the farm for the old dad; guess Squire'd part all right if I could pass him enough. As for the old woman, there's just no end to what I'd do—glad rags and brooches, and help all round the house. It'd be just Heaven and Witham Gala, playing

Providence to the old woman! . . . That's what
I want my brass for, when I strike it rich!" '

'A fool's dream!' Sarah said.

'A fine fool's dream.'

'Them as dreams over much likely never does
nowt else.'

He leaned forward still farther, the smile more
urgent on his lips. 'There was only one thing
used to fret him,' he went on, 'and he spent a
powerful lot of time thinking about it, and wearing himself thin. "S'pose she don't know me
when I sail in?" he used to say. "S'pose I'm
that changed I might as well be any other
mother's son as well as hers? There's a mighty
pile o' years between us—big, terrible years! I'd
sure break my heart if she didn't know me right
off, even if I'd grown a face like a pump-handle
and a voice like a prize macaw! But I guess I
needn't trouble," he used to say, "because
mothers always know. I've got that slick by heart
—they always know." ' He waited a moment,
and then pressed on, with a note that was like
alarm. 'Say, he was right, wa'n't he?' he asked
anxiously—'dead right? It's a sure thing that
mothers always know?'

The force of his demand seemed almost to
shake the obstinate figure so cynically aloof. It
was as if he were prompting her to something
that she knew as well as he, but would not admit
for some reason of her own. Even after he had
stopped speaking the demand seemed to persist,
and she answered at last with a cold smile on her
hard face.

'Nay, my lad,' she said sneeringly, 'you needn't
put yourself about! Eliza'll be fain to see you,

wherever you got your brass. She'll know you well enough, never fret, wi' yon pack o' cards in your hand!'

His smile died as if she had struck him—the whole laughing pleasure of him died. 'I worked for it honest,' he said in reply, but his voice sounded dull and tired. Even in the dusk she might have seen the spirit go out of him, the lines in his face deepen, his head sink, his shoulders droop. The merry boy that had come into the house was gone, leaving the stern man of middle age. Sarah could not see what she had done to him, but she could feel the change. Scenes with Jim in the old days had always ended much as this. Many a time he had come to her full of affection and fun, and in a few moments she had slain them both. He had looked up at her with hurt eyes that still laughed because they couldn't do anything else, and had held to his old cry— 'I'm *your* lad *really*, Aunt Sarah—same as Geordie is!'

He sat for a few minutes staring at the floor, his pipe with its filled bowl hanging idly from his hand. He seemed to be adjusting himself to new ideas, painfully making room for them by throwing overboard the old. Then he rose to his feet with a half-sigh, half-yawn—and laughed. Sarah heard him, and started—it was so like the old-time Jim! But though she might have winced in the old days, it did not trouble her, now. If she had had no tenderness for the scapegrace lad she was not likely to pity the grown, successful man. . . . Without looking at her again he went across to the window and stared out. The pane swung open wide on its bent rod, and not a breath of wind troubled its buckled frame. Across the vanished sands the light still glowed from the 'Ship,' red on the dark that seemed like a mere dissolution of everything into mist.

'Old Fleming still at the "Ship"?' he enquired, keeping his back turned. 'And May?' His voice warmed again on the little name. 'May's married this many a year, I guess!'

'Nay, not she!' Sarah said. 'She's not wed, nor like to be.' Unconsciously she relaxed a little. 'She was always terble sweet on Geordie, was May.'

The man looking out smiled at the light as if it had been a face. He spoke low, as if speaking to himself.

'I'd sure forgot!'

'I reckon she's waiting for him yet, but I doubt she'll wait till the Judgment, and after that!'

'She was always a sticker, was May. . . .' He swung round, cheerful again, though lacking the ecstasy with which he had come in. 'Sweet on Geordie, was she? Well, I guess a live dog's better than a dead lion! I'll hop across for a chin.'

'You'll loss yourself, crossing t'sand.'

'I've crossed it every night in my dreams!' He came back to her, with his face tender again, the thin flame of the candle showing his pleasant eyes and kindly lips. 'Say, though!' he added anxiously. 'I can come back?'

'Best bide at t' "Ship."'

'But I'd a deal rather sleep here!'

'Well, you wain't, and that's flat!'

'There's Geordie's bed, ain't there?' he urged her, in pleading tones. 'I'll lay you've kept it fixed for him all along!'

'Ay—for Geordie!' said Geordie's mother, setting her mouth.

'Couldn't you kinder think I was Geordie once in a while?'

'Nay.'

'Not for a mite of a minute?' His voice shook.

'Nay, not I.'

He lifted his shoulders, and let them droop again. 'I'm sure coming back, though!' he finished, in his persistent way. . . . 'Stop a shake, though! What about the tide?'

His eyes turned from old custom to the table over the hearth, and, crossing over to it, he struck a light. The silver box in his hand flashed a tiny scintilla on the dusky air. He looked up at the table, but he did not see it, the match dwindling above his brooding face.

'You might ha' been just a mite glad to see me!' he exclaimed wistfully, stamping it out upon the flags. 'Why, you'd never ha' known me from Adam if I hadn't given you the call! It'll give me the knock right out if May don't know me neither when I sail in. They say sweethearts don't forget, no more than mothers, but perhaps it's all a doggoned lie!'

'She was Geordie's lass—not yours!' Sarah told him, with jealous haste.

'Sure!' he said with a smile, and struck a second match.

Now he looked at the table in earnest, but only for a space. 'Saturday,' she heard him murmuring, in an absent voice. 'Martinmas, ain't it? . . . Tide at ten. . . .'

She made a movement forward and put out her hands.

'Nay, but yon's never——' she began; and stopped.

'Eh, old woman?'

'Nay, it's nowt.'

'It's Saturday, ain't it?'

'I reckon it is.'

'Saturday's my day for luck,' she heard him saying, as the match died down. 'I've got a cinch on Saturdays, that's sure!' The gaiety in his tone was only a mockery of what it had been before. 'Tide at ten, eh?—and it's six, now.' He drew his watch from his pocket and gave it a glance. 'Well, so long! I'll be right back!'

To both the moments seemed endless in which he moved across the floor. His look dwelt upon her in a last effort to reach her heart, and then lingered about the room on the dim fellowships of his youth. But even Geordie himself could hardly have touched her in that hour. The strongest motive that had ruled her life had her finally by the throat.

Yet she called to him even as he went, afraid, woman-like, of the sound of the shut door. 'Jim!' she flung after him. 'Jim, lad! . . . Jim!'

'Say! Did you call?' He was back again on wings.

'Nay . . . it was nowt.' She indicated the pocket-book within reach of her hand. 'You'd best take yon truck along wi' you an' all.'

Even in his disappointment he was still able to smile. 'It don't need a safe between it and a Thornthet, I guess!' was all he said. In that moment, indeed, the money was nothing and less than nothing to them both. Sarah was honest to the core, and never remembered once that dead men tell no tales and that the sea does not betray. . . . The thing that had conquered her soul was at least also above that.

'Ten, wa'n't it?' he asked, drifting reluctantly out again. His voice came from farther away, like the gull's voice from the sky. 'So long! Cheerio! I'll be back again with the tide. . . .'

IV

SHE heard rather than felt the silence re-enfold the house, like the swish of a curtain softly tumbled down. She was vividly on the alert for every change in the brooding quiet, but she was not afraid of the inevitable sound that must shortly break it again. To herself she seemed to be shut into the very heart of things, where every one knows his secret hiding-place to be. Nothing could hurt her there, because it was shut away from pain. Neither remorse nor fear could touch her in that calm.

Yet all the time her mind had followed the man who had gone out, hearing the thud of his feet on the sandy ground, and seeing the bulk of him huge on the sea-wall. The sound of his feet would be sharper on the beach, but when he got to the sand it would be muffled as if with cloths. When he came to the channel he would stand and hail, and the light from the 'Ship' would lie on the water like a road. . . .

But never to-night or in all time would he get as far as the bank. Suddenly, as he walked, he would hear a whisper out of the west. It would mean nothing to him at first, nor the wind feeling along his cheek. He would say to himself only that the trees were astir on the far point.

Then he would hear a noise like a coming shower, and lift up his face to meet the first of the rain. But the sound that came after would come running along the sand, until every rib was vibrating its message to his feet. When he knew what it was, he would stand perfectly still, and then he would spring in the air and start to run. But, run as he might, he would never reach the shore, or stand on the old road that would take him over to May. The white tide-horses were swifter far than he; their unshod hoofs would outrun his heavy boots. The sweeping advance-water would suddenly hem him in, swirling before his feet and shooting behind his back. He would run this way and that in the dark, but it would be no use. He would run and run, but it would never be any use. . . .

From complete detachment she passed gradually to a comforting sense of quittance and ease. It was as if a burden that she had carried all her life had been cut away, so that she could lift up her head and look in front of her and breathe free. The sickening jealousy was gone, the gnawing pain at her heart, the fierce up-swelling of destructive rage, the long, narrowed-down brooding of helpless hate. Never again would she be able to see herself as the poor relation fawning at Eliza's skirts. The thing had been done at last which paid Eliza in full.

She had, as she came back within range of feeling again, one last, great moment of exultant pride. She seemed to herself actually to grow in size, to tower in the low room as the shadow of the homecomer had towered over ceiling and wall. Into the hands of this oppressed and poverty-stricken woman there had suddenly been given the heady power of life and death, and the stimulant of it was like wine in her thin blood, making her heart steady as a firm-blown forge. She felt strong enough in that moment to send every child of Eliza's out to its death in the maw of the night wave. She felt an epic figure poised on the edge of the world, heroic, tremendous, above all laws. Indeed, she seemed, as it were, to be the very Finger of God itself. . . .

And then faintly the exaltation sank; dimmed, rather, as on a summer day the sharpness goes out of the high lights on lawn and wall. The sun is not gone, but the farthest and finest quality of it is suddenly withdrawn. In some such way a blurring of vivid certainties came upon her brain. A breath of wind was blown sharply through the open window, and with a touch of surprise she found that she was cold. The fire, so lately encouraged by the visitor's presence, had died sulkily into grey clinkers tinged with red that had no more warmth to it than a splash of paint. The candle, on the other hand, had sprung into a tall flame from a high wick. It was as if it was making a last effort to illumine the world for the woman over whose mind was creeping that vague and blurring mist.

With the slackening of the mental tension her physical self slackened, too. She began to rock to and fro, muttering softly as she swayed.

'Blind thoughts in a blind body's brain!' she was saying to herself. . . . 'Ay, it's about time. A blind night and a blind tide. . . . Ay, it's about time. . . .'

And yet through the blind night and with her

blind sight she still saw the figure swinging over the sands, broad, confident, strong, as were all at Blindbeck—successful and rich. Always her mind kept close at its back, seeing the solid print of it on the air, feeling the muscular firmness of its tread, and hearing the little whistled tune that kept escaping between its teeth. . . .

Suddenly she raised her voice, as if addressing somebody a long way off.

'What d'you want wi' a bed as'll never sleep in bed again? Nay, my lad, you'll have nowt but churchyard mould! . . . Yon's if they find him, when the tide comes in. There'll be a bonny fairing for Eliza when the tide comes in!'

She stopped abruptly as Simon clattered into the room, holding herself motionless by a final effort of will. He glanced uneasily at the still figure, the unspread table and the dead fire, but he did not speak. He was still conscious of guilt and ready to make amends, even to the extent of going supperless to bed. Outside the door, he had felt curiously certain that Sarah was not alone, and even now he looked into corners for figures that were not there. Coming in from the dark on the marsh, his instinct had told him instantly that the atmosphere had changed, but the knowledge faded, once he was well inside. He wondered whether anything had been done with the milk, but did not like to ask; and, setting the still-lighted lantern on the floor, stooped to unloose his boots.

'All yon talk about Geordie's fair give me the jumps!' he remarked suddenly, with an embarrassed laugh. 'I could ha' sworn I heard his voice as I was snecking shippon door!'

She did not answer, and with an inward curse at his own foolishness he bent lower over his boots. 'Another o' yon big tides,' he went on hurriedly, when the thongs were loosed. 'It's sharp on t'road now. I could hear it as I come in.'

Even as he spoke the room was suddenly filled with the sound of the sea. Before the majesty of the coming presence the whole house seemed to cringe and cower. Sarah felt the room swing round with her, and caught at the table, gripping the edge of it until her very fingers seemed of wood.

'There it be!' Simon said, raising himself. 'It's big, as I said.' He clanked across to the window as he spoke, the laces slapping and trailing on the flags; and again, as he put his face to the square, the wind that blows before the tide stirred mightily through the room. Far-off, but coming fast, they could hear the messenger from the deep, sweeping its garment over the head of the crouched waste, as it sped to deliver its challenge at the locked gate of the sea-wall.

Sarah had still control over her actual body, but no more. With Simon's entrance she had realised herself again, and knew that she was weak and old, with a mind that had got beyond her, and cried and ran to and fro as Jim would run when he heard the Wave. Always she seemed to herself to be close at his back, but now she ran to warn him and stumbled as she ran. She flung out her arms towards him in an aching passion to hold him close, and in that moment felt the truth drop, stilly, into her whirling brain. He turned his face towards her swiftly as they went, and for all its likeness it was not Jim's face. She